the
LEFT HAND
of **D O G**

A deeply heartfelt story ... Clarke understands the peculiar magic that is addressing a serious topic without taking oneself seriously in the process, and wields wit and wordplay with enviable skill. Pratchett and Adams fans, take note.

- *TYLER HAYES, AUTHOR OF* THE IMAGINARY CORPSE

Farcical theatre at its best ... full of wit and charm.

- JOHN DEREK, GOODREADS USER

A wonderfully accessible yarn.

- SIESTA, GOODREADS USER

What a fun book!

- JIM RAZINHA, GOODREADS USER

A perfect way to spend a stormy evening.

- MARGARET, GOODREADS USER

For everyone whose mind is reeling from, well, everything and who can't cope with another serious novel about serious people dealing with serious problems. Not right now.

THE LEFT HAND OF DOG

AN EXTREMELY SILLY TALE OF ALIEN ABDUCTION

SI CLARKE

The Left Hand of Dog

Print edition ISBN 978-1-9162878-5-3

ebook edition ISBN 978-1-9162878-6-0

www.whitehartfiction.co.uk

Most recent update: 25 July 2021

Editing by:

- Lucy York of Lucy Rose York
- Nicholas Taylor of Just Write Right
- Hannah McCall of Black Cat Editorial Services

Cover illustration by: Tom Edwards

Black and white illustration by: Ricardo Mossini

❀ Created with Vellum

This book is written in British English. If you're used to reading American English, some of the spelling and punctuation may seem unusual. I promise, it's totally safe.

This story also features a number of Canadianisms. Sadly, I cannot promise these are safe. You may find yourself involuntarily wearing a touque and craving Timbits and a double-double. It can't be helped. Seek treatment immediately.

Lastly, this book contains an inordinate number of geek culture references. This as an homage to all things science fiction. There are countless references to all my favourites – *Star Trek*, *Red Dwarf*, *Firefly*, *The X-Files*, *Doctor Who*, *Battlestar Galactica*, *Hitchhiker's Guide to the Galaxy*, *Babylon 5*, *The Expanse*, etc. None of it should be read as derogatory or dismissive, nor would I ever suggest my work can take the place of anyone else's. Please support artists and authors. This is my love song to the entire genre.

This work contains the following:

- Anaphylactic shock
- Minor injury to a dog

Also, please note that trans women are women. Trans men are men. Non-binary people are who they tell you they are. This book is not for TERFs.

'I just want to be the kind of person who has adventures, you know? That was the whole point of moving to Canada. And it's why we're here now. Away from Toronto, I mean. We deserve to have an interesting life, don't you think?'

Spock gave me her full, rapt attention – head tilted to one side in that stereotypical confused German shepherd pose.

It was the first day of our week-long getaway in Algonquin Park. Overhead, the velvety blackness was interrupted only by pinpricks of stars. At my feet, the Oxtongue River made soothing, bubbling noises.

'This is perfect.' I glanced at my watch – nine o'clock. 'Well, what do you think, Spock? Shall we call it a night?'

———

Back in our little log cabin, I cracked open a can of Bean Me Up espresso milk stout by Fuggles & Warlock and called up a book on my phone. Catherynne Valente's *Space Opera* had been on my TBR list for ages, but I never seemed to find the time. Taking a sip of the beer, I read the first paragraph ... and promptly fell asleep.

'Geez, Spock, you want me to freeze to death?' I tried to grab some of the duvet and ... wondered why I couldn't move. I opened my eyes, but it was too dark to see.

'Hang on,' I muttered. 'You sleep at my feet. Why are you stealing my covers?' *Surely my eyes should have started adapting to the darkness by now.* I tried to move my hand again. No joy on my right; it was pinned in place. My left arm was tangled around Spock, her fur thick between my fingers. I lifted my hand to my face and used my nose to tap my watch to activate the torch – and promptly began hyperventilating.

This wasn't my house. *No, wait.* I wasn't at home. Spock and I had gone away somewhere. My mind felt like it was swimming through treacle – my reactions were sluggish and my head was foggy.

And now we were spooned together in some sort of double-wide coffin. No room to move. I was curled up on my side with a squishy gel supporting me. It felt cool and slick, like it ought to be liquid, but acted more like memory foam.

'I'm dreaming. I'm not trapped. It's just a dream.' Closing my eyes again, I took slow, deep breaths.

Two, three, five. I struggled to remember what came after five. *Seven, eleven, thirteen.* Another deep breath.

We'd left Toronto and gone… *Where did we go?*

Some sort of back-to-nature break – that was it.

Spock tried to roll over.

We both panicked at the same time – her scrabbling desperately and me screaming. A light appeared beyond what turned out to be a clear roof above us. Although I couldn't make out what was outside the confines of our little prison, I could at least see that there *was* an outside. *That's comforting, I suppose.*

'Algonquin Park! That's where we were.' We'd gone hiking and then we'd retired for the night in a little log cabin.

I sat upright as the lid of the coffin lifted and slid aside with a soft *kshhh*. Wave after wave of nausea made me wish I hadn't moved. Spock made that *hur-hur-hur* that was both a motion and a noise. I scrambled to one end of the coffin just as she threw her dinner up at the other end.

A pink ball of fuzz in the corner of the coffin-box caught my eye. I reached out and picked it up. Spock's brain. A handmade squeaky toy shaped like a human brain. I'd bought it for her a year earlier. She carried it with her everywhere. She must have been clutching it in her sleep when we … when … when *whatever* had happened. Spock snatched it out of my hands.

I looked around the dim room. Maybe a workshop? *No, too clean for that. A dentist's office?* Lots of shelves, cupboards, and bits of strange equipment.

Spock sat back on her haunches and panted. I wrapped my arms around her. 'We'll be all right, mate. Just gotta figure it out.'

A few months back, I'd packed up my dog and everything I owned. I'd moved us from England to Canada. It was all part of my grand plan to reinvent myself. Ergo the hiking: I was determined to become the kind of person who had adventures.

Finding myself in an alien dentist's office wasn't really the sort of adventure I had in mind, though.

Startled by the sound of movement behind me, I whirled around to face three ... they had to be children in bunny costumes. 'What?' That's what they had to be, right? I mean, they weren't actually rabbits. Definitely not. For one thing, they stood upright. *Real bunnies don't normally do that, do they?* For another, they were about the size of Spock.

But the costumes looked real in that no skin showed through – not even on their faces – and I couldn't see any zips. Also, I was pretty sure rabbits didn't come in pastel rainbow colours. Actually, they reminded me of a toy I'd had as a child. *Bunnyboo*, I'd called it. Four-year-old me was terribly inventive.

'Check out your floopy-floppy ears! How adorable are you?' *Nervous sarcasm still intact then.*

I was nauseated enough that shaking my head seemed like a bad idea. 'It was beer I had last night, right? Not, like, psychedelic mushrooms? Maybe some natural tree spore that makes a person have trippy visions?' No one answered me. Or even looked at me.

Spock sat neatly and dropped her brain in my lap. She lifted a paw towards the nearest of the bunnyboos – for want of a better word. The creature's mint green fur matched the emerald hue of its humongous Disney princess eyes. 'Yip,' said Spock in her smallest, most polite voice.

This is not happening. I must be dreaming. Or hallucinat-ing. Something.

The creature pulled a device from a holster like a carpen-ter's apron and pointed it at Spock. Or maybe it was merely reading what was on the screen – if it even had a screen. Who was I kidding? I had no idea what they were doing.

Another, slightly taller bunnyboo – this one periwinkle blue with eyes like Wedgewood plates – stepped forwards and 'spoke' to Spock as well. That is, its mouth moved and Spock's full attention was on it. But no sound emerged. Spock yipped again in response to whatever it was I couldn't hear.

Spock pointed at me with her long, sable nose then looked back at the bunnyboos and emitted a low noise, not quite a growl.

'Would someone please tell me what the bollocking pufferfish is going on here?' I demanded. Okay, not demanded. Requested. Well, pleaded. Whined, maybe. Whatever verb it was I verbed, no one paid me any heed.

The bunnyboos of my strange hallucination were too deeply engrossed in their silent conversation with my very real dog to spare me any of their attention. It was like watching a TV on mute – except I could hear movements and breathing and the sound of my heart beating a drum on the inside of my chest.

After a few further moments of this bizarre fever dream, Spock leapt down out of the coffin and turned to face me. She sat on her haunches and looked me in the eye. Then she lifted one paw at me in a clear imitation of the 'stay' command I used with her.

A bunnyboo with heather purple fur lowered a rope lead over Spock's head. Spock stood and followed them from the room.

'Where are you taking my dog, you fluffy bastards?' I clambered out of the coffin-bed and scrabbled after them as fast as my besocked feet would carry me. But the thick metal door slid shut seconds before I got to it.

I pounded impotently on the door, screaming, 'Spock! Come back. Don't let those fuzzy arseholes hurt you.' Unable to find a doorknob or control panel or anything, I leant against the wall next to the door and slid down until I landed on my arse. I shivered and hugged my knees to my chest.

Why can't I wake up? Letting my head fall forwards, I cried for a bit, whimpering Spock's name periodically.

After a while, I took a deep breath. And another. I counted primes up to thirty-one.

'Time to snap out of it, Lem. Think, think, think. If this is a dream, you'll wake up soon enough, have a nice shower, go for a hike, maybe later you'll get some therapy – and everything will be fine. But if it's not a dream, and you really have been kidnapped by small furry creatures, then you need your wits about you, right?'

I'd read somewhere that talking to yourself didn't mean you were crazy – it was only crazy if you answered yourself.

'Right,' I replied. 'Okay, first things first.' I checked my smartwatch. Where the date and time normally were, there was just a single word: ERROR.

Hmm, that's weird. I checked the relevant settings. *Offline. I suppose that was to be expected.*

Deep breath. 'Right, let's check this place out.' I hauled myself to my feet and looked around, stopping to grab Spock's brain toy. I clutched it to myself as I explored the perfectly ordinary room. The walls were a brilliant, glossy white and the shiny, clean floor was pale grey.

The ceiling was more than two metres high, but the door Spock and the bunnyboos had walked through had a clearance of well under two metres – I'd have to duck to walk through it.

The tops of the bunnyboos' ears barely reached my shoulders, so that fit. The edges of the space were lined with cupboards and worktops – all sized for beings much shorter than me.

There was something that looked like a sink. Smacking my lips, I wondered how long it had been since I'd had anything to drink or eat. How long had I been unconscious?

A series of coffins on plinths stood in the middle of the room – not just the one Spock and I had climbed out of. Four of them. They looked a bit like commercial fridges lying on their backs. I approached the nearest one and peered in. The top was frosted over. I touched it to see if it was cold – but then the room was like a giant refrigerator. Everything felt cold.

I focused on looking through the window rather than just at it. There was something in there. Another person, maybe? It dawned on me to use my watch's torch again, so I switched it on and aimed my wrist at the window. I gazed into the abyss and … a large yellow bird stared back at me.

It opened its beak and screamed. Well, I *thought* it screamed – much like when the bunnyboos spoke, I couldn't hear anything. I could definitely hear myself howling, so I knew my ears worked.

The door to the room whooshed open with considerably more urgency than it had whooshed shut with. The three bunnyboos and Spock ran back in.

Oh, thank God!

The purple one still held Spock's lead. Thankfully, she didn't look any the worse for whatever they'd done. I ran to her. Dropping to my knees, I wrapped my arms around her neck and buried my hands in her thick fur. 'My baby. Are you okay?' She sat on the floor and leant her head into my chest.

The lid of the coffin-fridge I'd disturbed slid open and the bunnyboos gathered around it. They had their backs to us. This was my chance. I lifted the end of the lead up over Spock's head, then beckoned her to follow me as I ran for the door.

As before, it slid shut before I got to it. I skidded to a halt in my sock-feet and slammed into the closed door. You know that definition of stupidity that involves repeating the same actions and expecting a different outcome? Yeah, well, I may or may not have searched for a doorknob in the same spots I'd already examined. But what else was I supposed to do?

Hearing footsteps behind me, I turned to find the blue one was pointing a device at me. Weapon? Communicator? Weather-sensor? Coaster? How the hell was I supposed to know?

Blue looked at me. Green raised her arms. *Wait, his arms? Their arms?* I shook my head. *Not the time to wonder about alien pronouns.* I decided to stick with she until someone told me otherwise.

Blue's lips moved rapidly. But with no noise. The bird-creature stood up in its coffin and squawked. Frantically.

Spock leapt in front of me. Alsatian genes told her to protect me. In stressful situations, they tended to override any good sense in her tiny dog brain.

The bunnyboos had a silent conversation. Looked heated, though.

'Wrooh.' Spock made a plaintive bark.

Didn't work. Blue moved towards me. The Killer Rabbit of Caerbannog raced through my mind. But a dog-shaped shield flew through the air and chomped down on her child-sized leg. She pulled the bunnyboo away. Then, it was all a blur. Fur flew in every direction. Green. Blue. Purple. Spock's sable. Limbs and bodies tumbled and rolled. Spock snarled and snapped her teeth.

Green pointed her device at my dog. Spock crumpled like an empty bag. My vision glowed red. Not literally, of course. Figuratively. Still…

'You killed my best friend, you fuzzy little bastard. I'll kill you all, you monsters.' I launched myself at the nearest bunnyboo, whichever arsehole it was. The last thing I saw was the same weapon being pointed at me. Then something hit me and I died.

Okay, so I wasn't dead. I was warm and comfortable, though, which persuaded me to stay in bed a bit longer. Somewhere, at the edge of my memory, I recalled a strange dream. *What was it about?*

Bunnies! There were talking bunnies and a giant parrot and an alien dentist's office. Frak me, what was I drinking last night?

The mattress was cushier than mine, so I figured I must still be in the little cottage near Algonquin Park. Spock's weight pressed on the back of my knees.

It must have been late morning, as I could sense brightness. 'Ugh, Spock. You're not going to believe the dream I had.' I rolled over onto my back and opened my eyes.

It wasn't the cottage. Spock and I were in a bright white room. She wore a new collar – turquoise with pale yellow polka dots. 'What's going on?' As if she was likely to answer me.

She inched closer and set her pink plush brain toy down on the bed next to me. 'Lem no panic.'

And that's precisely when I freaked the frak out. 'Don't tell me not to panic, Spock. Why the hell shouldn't I panic?

I've been kidnapped and murdered by alien bunnies and now I'm in prison with my dog telling me not to freak. What's to not wig out about?' The room began to spin around me as I hyperventilated.

Spock lay down and whined as she pressed herself against me. 'No panic. Everything okay.' The voice reminded me, weirdly, of my dad – who'd died when I was sixteen.

My watch face no longer showed an error. Instead, it declared: SPOCK SPEAKING.

'A bold claim.' I sat up and leant against the pillow as the room swam around me. Spock whimpered. 'Everything is very much not okay, Spock. Hang on.' I giggled hysterically for an age or two.

'Oh my gosh. Someone had me going there for a sec. That whine came from you, Spock. I heard it … I heard it. Whoever I've been speaking to – the voice is coming from my watch.' Whatever drugs were swimming through my blood clearly had a hallucinogenic effect.

The screen altered as I spoke: LEM SPEAKING.

'All right, you wisecracking bastards. That's enough. No more taking the piss. Who am I *really* speaking to?'

Spock pawed at my arm like she did when she wanted me to pet her. 'Rub chest.'

SPOCK SPEAKING, lied my watch.

I patted her chest – not because some joker on the other end of the line told me to do so, but because the real, living Spock the Dog clearly wanted me to. And it felt good to do so. She had a calming effect on me.

'I don't know what's happening or where we are or who's pretending to be you. But I love you, Spock.' I took a deep breath and considered my options. There weren't many.

'Spock loves Lem,' said … someone who definitely wasn't my Alsatian.

'Okay, mate.' Whoever they were, they were obviously listening to me. Probably had cameras watching us as well. 'I hope there's a toilet somewhere because I really have to wee.'

Spock pointed with her nose to a door behind the head of the bed. 'Pee place.'

'All right, doofus. You're definitely not the one talking but I'll go check it out.' I got up and headed to where Spock had indicated.

The door was too low for me to walk through but it slid open as I approached. I ducked into the small space, which was indeed a bathroom. Everything looked clean and high-tech – except the toilet was just a hole in the white floor. I shrugged and did what I had gone in there for. To my left was what appeared to be a shower and to my right was an ordinary bathroom sink. Lower to the ground, though – like it was designed for kids.

I remembered the bunnyboos. If they had existed, that is – which they definitely did not and they certainly hadn't murdered me and/or my dog. But if they *had* existed, then the sink would probably be sized for them.

As I washed my hands, I studied myself in the mirror. My dark blond hair looked like I'd not combed or washed it in a week.

I decided a shower probably wasn't the worst idea, so I stripped off my pyjamas and hopped in. The water was, of course, aimed at about my navel. I had to crouch down to clean my face and hair. Afterwards, I reached for the – *Bollocks!* No towel. Or clean clothes. 'Oops. I guess the *Hitch-hiker's Guide* was right after all. That'll teach me.' But I was hit by a gust of warm air – up to my chest. I ducked down and tried to let it blast some of the water out of my hair.

I put my pyjamas back on and returned to the … bedroom? Hospital room? Prison cell?

Spock was still lounging on the bed. She looked up at me and farted – nice to know some things never changed. 'Feed Spock?' She wagged her tail hopefully. Maybe it really was her talking.

'I got nothing, mate. Sorry.'

Spock sighed melodramatically and flopped down on the bed.

I looked around. The only door was the one to the bathroom. The room was a rectangle. *No, what's the word for a four-sided space where the sides aren't equal?* The two long walls were equal in length but not quite parallel. The wall behind the bed was wider than the wall opposite it. The bed was square, maybe one and a half metres. If I wanted to stretch out, tough – but I normally curled up in a ball, so it hadn't bothered me thus far.

The only other furniture was a low table in one corner of the room. Aside from the bathroom door, the walls were plain white and featureless.

'Wait.' The opposite wall had a frame around it – like one massive door frame. I tapped it. 'Huh.' I tapped the wall to my right. 'Huh,' I repeated. I headed over to the wall across the room. And then the one behind the bed. 'Huh,' I said for a completely unnecessary third time.

Spock lifted her head and looked at me. 'What do?'

'Listen.' I tapped the wall behind the bed again, then circled the room, tapping all four walls in various spots. When I knocked on the wall opposite the bed—

'Not same,' said Spock, joining me at the wall.

'Prisoners to step away from the door,' boomed a voice from my watch. It wasn't Spock this time. We both jumped away from the wall.

I looked at my wrist. PURPLE BUNNYBOO SPEAKING.

'No way,' I shouted. 'No. There's no way your name is

actually Purple Bunnyboo.' You might say I wasn't adapting very well to this – whatever this new experience was. I was still pretty sure I was dreaming. But it was a hell of a detailed dream.

A small door opened in the framed wall, maybe half a metre wide and half that in height. A tray with two bowls and two mugs was pushed through. 'We have analysed your nutritional requirements and provided food that meets it,' said the deep, gravelly voice. The door swung shut and disappeared.

'Would now be a convenient time for me to introduce myself?' said a new voice.

I stared at my watch: UNIVERSAL TRANSLATOR / PERSONAL AI SPEAKING. I'd never had any kind of app like that on my watch. Had someone tampered with it?

I looked at the food. Spock was quite keen to eat. I lifted the tray and carried it to the low table. 'How am I supposed to know which is which?' I asked no one in particular. 'Does it even matter?'

'The bowl on your left has been designed to meet your needs,' said the universal translator. 'The one on the right has a higher protein content, aligning to Spock's needs. The mugs are empty, but you can fill them from the tap in the bathroom.' It sounded like one of those text-to-speech programs. Just words. No real personality.

'What is it? And who the hell are you? What is this place? Who are these frakking bunnyboos? What the bollocking hell are we doing here? How did we even get here?'

While I bombarded my watch with questions, Spock waited impatiently – a steady flow of drool pooling at her feet. 'Feed Spock, please.'

I lifted the lid off the indicated dish. The contents looked like a sort of grey risotto, but the scent that hit my nose made my mouth water almost as much as Spock's was. 'Sweet potato vindaloo? Really?' I was sceptical of eating anything in this strange prison. But then, if this was all just a grand hallucination, what difference would it make if I imagined myself eating food? Besides, I was famished.

And so was Spock, obviously. 'Give.'

'It's what your friend's mind had flagged as favourite,' said the universal translator.

'My friend's... You're reading our minds? Hang on... Are you sure that's not mine?'

'It has been formulated to meet her nutritional requirements,' replied the disembodied voice. 'The ship's facilities prepared a meal of the appropriate nutrients and calories for each of you and then seasoned them with your favourite flavours.'

Ship? What ship? And then I just ... gave up. I decided to go along with the dream, or the hallucination, or the prank, or whatever the bastarding hell this whole thing was. With a shrug, I set the bowl on the floor for Spock, who inhaled the contents. I lifted the lid off the other bowl. It looked like the same drab porridge. I sniffed it. 'What is it?'

'It is 500 calories' worth of nutrient porridge, comprising thirty grams of protein, eighteen grams of fat, twenty—' said the voice I was beginning to hate.

'Yeah, yeah, all right. But what is it? And why does it smell like ... that?'

'It is made using the root of [no frame of reference] combined with [no frame of reference]. The seasonings are created from chemical compounds designed to emulate your preferred foods. Whereas Spock's mind showed a clear favourite, yours contained 243 foods all flagged as favourites, so the computer selected two at random.'

No frame of what? I took a tentative bite. 'Is that…' I tried to identify what I was eating. The lumpy, slimy texture wasn't helping the process. 'Mango?' I smacked my tongue a few times. 'And peanut butter?'

'Yes.'

The first bite made me realise how hungry I was, so I sat and wolfed the contents of the bowl down almost – but not quite – as quickly as Spock had eaten hers.

Now that I'd decided to play along with this – for the moment, at least – it was freeing. I could indulge my curiosity without letting my panic get the best of me. 'Hey, universal translator – actually, that's going to get old really quick. Is there anything else I can call you?'

'You may call me anything you like, Lem,' said my watch.

'Kay, fine. I hereby dub thee "Holly",' I said. 'So anyway, Holly?' Spock stood up and headed for the bathroom.

'Yes, Lem?'

HOLLY SPEAKING, declared my watch face.

I ran after Spock, hoping she wasn't going to pee everywhere – though I had no idea where she was supposed to do her business. Instead, I found her squatting over the hole in the floor. 'Oh, er, sorry, Spock.' I felt my face flush as I ducked and backed out of the bathroom.

'What the hell is wrong with me? I just apologised to my dog for seeing her do a wee – I've seen her wee every day since I got her.' I shook my head to clear it. 'Anyway, Holly, would it be possible to make a request to the kitchen?'

'Of course, Lem. Within reason.'

'Never mix mango and peanut butter again.'

As Holly answered 'noted,' the watch face changed – GREEN BUNNYBOO SPEAKING – and a big, booming voice announced, 'The prisoner in cell A will step forwards.'

Did they mean me? Was this cell A? How was I supposed to know?

I stood up and patted Spock's head as she joined me. 'You're such a good girl, Spock.'

A larger door – about a metre and a half in height – opened next to the smaller door the food tray had been shoved through. Green and Purple were both standing just the other side.

I bent down to duck through the door and stepped forwards, but Purple stabbed at me with some sort of truncheon. 'Not you. Step back.'

'What? You want to question my dog? What information do you think she has?'

Spock padded towards the door, clutching her brain between her teeth, then turned to face me. She dropped the toy at my feet. 'Lem no panic. Spock good girl.'

'No, no. I don't care. You can shoot me again if you want, but you're not taking my dog.' I stamped my foot like the disgruntled toddler I apparently was. Moving to stand in front of Spock, I put my hand on her.

Spock walked calmly around me, then turned to face me once again. 'Stay.' She walked out the door. It swung shut behind her, locking me alone in the cell. I slapped the wall pointlessly. The panic I'd staved off while Spock was still in the room was creeping back up my insides.

'Ow.' I rubbed my hand on the brushed cotton of my pyjama bottoms. 'What the hell am I supposed to do now?' I demanded of no one in particular.

'Please restate the question,' replied Holly.

As I paced the room, I demanded, 'Where the hell did those fluffy arseholes take Spock? I swear, if they hurt her, I … I …' I ground my teeth. 'I don't actually know what I'll do – but it won't be pretty.'

'Spock has been taken for questioning,' replied Holly. 'She will not be harmed.'

I forced my anger and frustration aside. As much as I was concerned for Spock, I wouldn't get anything by being belligerent. Instead, I needed to gather as much information as I could. 'Who are you, Holly? Why is it you're talking to me, but your friends are only interested in what Spock has to say?'

'To answer your first question, I am your personal translation and assistance device. I am equipped with basic AI functionality to help facilitate your understanding of reality. Translators sometimes communicate with one another at the request of their owners, but they don't normally speak to any other sentients. Your captors are most likely speaking to Spock about the crimes for which she has been arrested.'

I stopped in my tracks. 'Arrested? What do you mean arrested?' I tried to swallow the terror. It was hard to think rationally. 'What crimes are you suggesting my dog has committed? Is she going to be okay?'

'With regard to your first three questions, I'm sorry, but I'm not party to that information. As for her well-being, the [no frame of reference] convention of [no frame of reference] dictates that she not be harmed. She must be safely delivered to the court on [no frame of reference] to stand trial.'

'Okay, well, that's something at least. Sort of.' I closed my eyes. 'If Spock's the one who's been arrested, why are you talking to me, not her?'

'I am your translator and personal AI,' said what had been a perfectly ordinary smartwatch yesterday.

'Yeah, but why aren't you Spock's translator? You have to admit I've got you there, right?'

'Please restate the question.'

'Why were you assigned to me?' I opened my eyes and stared at the featureless wall in front of me. There was almost certainly a camera somewhere, though I couldn't see one.

'Each individual who doesn't already have a translator is assigned one. I was installed on your watch. Spock didn't have a device suitable for an AI, so one was given to her.' That explained the new collar, at least. 'It was fitted with an identical translator – though, over time, the differences between AI units increase as they adapt to their owners' preferences.'

That made me sit up. 'So, this whole time you've been speaking to me, you've also been talking to Spock. Well, not you – but an identical you. How come I couldn't hear anyone talking to her?'

The answer hit me a split second before Holly spoke. 'Because, much like the bunnyboos, Spock's device speaks at a frequency not detectable by human ears.'

'Huh,' was all that I could muster as I flopped down onto the bed, dejected. Spock had been gone for a while. Despite Holly's assurances that she was okay, I was worried. The anxiety felt like a rock in my chest.

'Initially, you can set me in either literal or figurative mode,' said Holly. 'Over time, I'll learn your personal preferences for how best to relay information to you.'

I scrunched up my face. 'What do you mean?'

My personal AI did not sigh at me. It definitely didn't. 'At present, I have not been set to either literal or figurative mode and I don't know enough of your preferences to make a reasonable guess, so there are gaps in our conversation where there is no common frame of reference available. If you instruct me to use literal mode, I will endeavour to explain alien concepts precisely to aid your acquisition of knowledge. If you set me to figurative, then – to facilitate expedient communications – I will choose the closest corollary, drawing from your own mind. This will include facts you already know but may have forgotten. I will also incorporate extrapolative and fictional sources. Your extensive knowledge of science fiction will provide a useful base for figurative mode.'

'Huh?'

'For instance, when you asked earlier about the composition of your meal, I could have explained that the primary bulk was derived from the root of a plant native to the fourth planet of a star system you have no name for in the galaxy you think of as NGC 5128. The root is known for providing complex carbohydrates and for its ability to absorb flavours. Or I could have said it was cassava. This would not have been factual in a literal sense – but it would have conveyed a basic understanding with fewer words.'

'Oh, yeah. Do that then, please. The figurative thing.' Although I was nauseated by my fear for Spock, I couldn't help but be fascinated by all the information that I was being fed. And more than a bit overwhelmed.

'As you wish,' said Holly.

The low door opened again and Spock returned, ears back and tail between her legs. She plodded to the edge of the bed. I reached for her, relief flooding my system. She buried her head in my armpit. 'Wanna go home.'

'Yeah, I know, mate. Me too.'

She looked up at me. 'Spock good girl?'

'The bestest,' I replied, stroking her fur. She climbed up onto the bed and nuzzled into me.

How were we ever going to get home?

Although I wanted to let her rest, I had to ask right away; she'd never remember if I waited. 'What happened, Spock?'

'Bunnyboos say "bad girl".' She covered her face with her paws.

I stroked her fur. 'You're a good girl, Spock.' Her tail gave a tentative little thump on the bed. 'What do they think you did?'

Spock whined. 'Say Spock bad girl.'

I twirled her velvety soft ears in my fingers. 'It's not true. You're a good girl – a very good girl.'

She wagged her tail more confidently and pressed her face into my hand. 'Rub cheeks.'

Spock didn't want to talk anymore. She refused to answer questions – instead, she curled herself into a ball, farted, and went to sleep.

I thought about asking Holly some more questions about where we were and how things were meant to work, but I didn't want to disturb Spock. Whatever had happened with the bunnyboos was clearly upsetting her.

Instead, I stroked her head and thought about how we

could get out of this situation. If I even believed the cocka-mamie story that Spock had been arrested, then surely we'd need a lawyer – someone to plead her case. And didn't they have to read us our rights? Why was I here – was I meant to be a witness to something?

And that was assuming this wasn't all some trippy dream or grand prank. I still wasn't entirely convinced.

After I'd been sitting quietly for a few minutes, the lights blinked out. 'Must be on a sensor,' I said aloud – forgetting I was trying not to disturb Spock. Out the corner of my eye, there was a flash of movement. Were the bunnyboos back? I sat up – and the lights came back on – but not before I freaked the frak out. Yes, again.

'Holly, what the bloody hell was that? What did I just see?' I wasn't screaming. Definitely not.

'Please restate the question.'

In my panic, I'd woken Spock. She leapt off the bed and looked around. 'Lem okay?'

'That wall,' I said, answering both Holly and the dog. I pointed at the framed wall opposite the bed. 'It disappeared. For a second, it wasn't there.'

'Are you asking about the window-wall, Lem?'

I glanced at my watch. It still weirded me out that Holly and Spock's voices both emanated from the same source.

'Er, yeah, Holly. I might be. I mean, what? It never occurred to you to mention this disappearing wall trick before?' Who was I supposed to glare at when my sarcasm was directed at a disembodied idiot chatbot? 'Holly, what's outside the window?'

'You are aboard the starship *Teapot*. This is the ship's holding cell area,' said the voice. 'The cells are clustered in a semicircle around an access point. There are five cells and a

corridor that leads to the medlab and a lift to other levels of
the ship.'

I nodded woodenly and stumbled towards the wall. That
made no sense. There was no way that I was on any kind of
spaceship. Maybe I was dreaming or hallucinating. Or I'd
been kidnapped. Perhaps this was all some elaborate prank.
I thought of the elaborate high jinks the office pranksters
got up— No. I shook my head. If I thought about it too
hard, I might break down entirely. 'How can I make it a
window again?' I wanted to see what else there was to this
place.

'The wall is opaque when the lights are on.'

I reached out and touched the wall, running my fingers
along its smooth surface. 'Okay, so I just have to stay still
long enough for the lights to switch off again.' I dropped
down to the floor and sat facing the wall.

Spock wandered over and joined me.

'No, Spock, we have to—'

'Make dark,' she said.

'That's not going to work, sweetie,' I told her. Except it
did. 'Oh, clever girl!' I reached up and patted her head.

The space on the other side of the window was clean and
white, like our cell. The lights were dim, just a narrow strip
of what looked like LEDs along the front of each cell. 'Ha!
There are other cells – other prisoners!'

'That is what I said,' said Holly.

Most of the cells had opaque white walls, but the one
across from mine was cast in deep shadow. Silhouetted
behind – or in front of, depending on the perspective – the
cell's big front window was a person sitting on the floor. They
sat like a human, but with a head more like you'd see on a
horse.

'Hello, talky friend,' said Spock. She tossed her brain at

the window. She ran to collect it after it bounced off and returned to sit next to me.

I twirled her ear in my hand. 'They can't hear you, sweetie. I'm sorry.'

Spock tilted her head and looked at me. 'Friend says hello.'

Holly cut into the conversation. 'The prisoner in cell E is requesting permission to communicate with you. Shall I put her through or decline the call?'

I raised my hand to my mouth so hard I accidentally slapped myself. Across the way, I saw the horse-person touch their own face – *her* face, apparently – in response.

'Yes, Holly, yes! Please put her through.' I stood up and straightened my hoodie out over my pyjama bottoms. I hoped I didn't have any of that horrid porridge on me – because this was proper first contact stuff.

'Hi,' said a feminine voice from my watch. 'Oh my gosh. You speak, too. That's amazing. Your – um – spouse has been telling me about you. She says you're awesome, by the way. Are you awesome? She and I met last night when they brought you in. You were unconscious, but Spock and I had a good old chat, didn't we? Well, I say we had a chat, but it's possible I did most of the talking. One of my dads is always telling me I need to let other people get a word in edgeways sometimes.'

The way she spoke reminded me of a woman I'd met at work a couple of days previously. Michelle. They even had the same voice. The absurdity of the situation combined with the bizarre déjà vu overwhelmed me. I was laughing and crying at the same time – snotting everywhere. The enormity and ridiculousness, paired with the mundane reminder of familiarity, finally cracked my mind like an eggshell.

'Oh, no, no,' said the horse-person. 'I'm sorry. Are you

okay? Do you need a doctor? Or, like, a priest or something? I'm sorry. I don't know your species. Is this normal? I just want to prepare myself so I know how to react. Please don't think I'm being rude – I don't mean to be. I just... Are you okay?'

I looked around but there weren't any tissues anywhere.

'Are you...? Do you need a towel to wipe your secretions away? There should be some in the cupboard under the sink where you do your ablutions. I'd get you one, but' – she flicked her head back and forth, her forelock flopping down over her face as she did so – 'you know ... prisoner.'

'Thanks,' I said. 'I didn't know there were towels.' I got to my feet, causing the lights to come on overhead. 'Back in a sec.'

She carried on talking. I walked towards the bathroom, still laughing and crying. Spock followed but turned back around when she saw where I was going. 'I might be here when you get back,' my fellow prisoner said. 'Never know, though. I might pop out to the shops for a bit. Was thinking I might pick up a roasted grass loaf for dinner.'

I splashed some water on my face, then pulled open the cupboard and grabbed a towel to dry myself off with. The horse-person – I really ought to find out her name – was still talking. 'Sorry, one of my other dads – not the same one I mentioned before – anyways, she always says people don't get my sense of humour.'

Returning to the main room, I asked Holly to switch off the lights and resumed my seat. 'Sorry about that. Just a bit overcome by my emotions there. Between being kidnapped and shot by aliens, and then waking up in prison on a space-ship and my dog telling me not to panic, and my watch suddenly giving lectures in linguistics and making first contact with an actual alien species, I guess I got a bit over-whelmed.'

My encounter with the bunnyboos was technically first contact – but they pretty much forced their presence on me. This was me voluntarily introducing myself to a new species. Spock circled the room and sat down next to me, leaning her whole body into me.

As I sat down on the floor in front of the window, the horse-person shifted into a different position, tucking her legs under herself. 'Yeah, I totally get that. Oh my gosh, I was at home, dreaming a new engine design when' – she lifted her arms in the air, waving two hooves around in a sort of lifting-whooshing motion – 'then I woke up in a stasis pod. Little bit disorientating, you know? I mean, I don't know about you, but I've never been kidnapped before. Not really, anyways. Well, there was that time that—'

She waved her hoofed arms as if to change direction. 'So, anyways, I was all, "Who are these bunnyboos and what do they want with you, [no frame of reference]?" That's what I asked myself. And then the interrogation session. That was a trip and a half – oh my gosh. Arrested? Held for trial. They've not questioned you yet, have they?' She was silhou-etted against the darkness of the, well, the brig.

'No, er, no one's questioned me or told me anything.' I wondered if I should get up and grab a pillow from the bed – my arse was going to get sore if I sat here too long. 'Sorry, I should've thought to introduce myself sooner. I'm Lem – er, I'm from Earth. This is my dog, Spock. What's your name?'

She did a bit of a double-take, jerking her head in rapid motions. 'Oh my gosh. You really are new. Have you honestly never had a universal translator before? I didn't think there were still people out there without them. It makes me wonder how people got by back in the olden days of interstellar travel. Like, can you imagine having to mime "Where is the toilet?" to someone who had a completely different anatomy? Or saying, "Hey, that thing you're eating sure does look tasty! Mind if I have a bite?" to someone who could digest something that was deadly poison to your species?'

I opened my mouth to respond but realised I didn't have a clue what to say. Besides, she wasn't finished.

'I'm sorry, I'm sorry. I should explain. I could tell you my name. It's [no frame of reference], if you're interested. But back in the early days of translators, programmers tried to transliterate names of people and places, but it was all "unintelligible noise this" and "awkward silence that". No, in the end, they decided the best thing for it was for people to make their own names for everyone they encounter. Once you assign a name to someone, your AI will remember it.'

The pieces started slotting into place in my brain. Sort of. 'So that's why it calls the bunnyboos … well, bunnyboos.' Spock sort of slid down where she was until she was lying on the ground.

The horse-person tapped her hoof on the ground in front of her. 'See, I don't hear what word you're actually using, because my AI translates it to my word for them. I named them after … um … I can't say the word or it'll translate it. It's like a mythical monster on my world. Like a scary Hallowe'en costume. And I gave Spock the name of my first lover. I don't know – something about her just reminds me of her. Anyways, I haven't decided what to call you. What about me? What are you going to call me?'

I blinked rapidly and leant back on my hands. 'I … er … I don't know.'

She flicked her head, pushing her mane down over her large forehead. 'Come on. It'll be good practice. You can talk through your process. Like, I was still a foal when I had to name my first alien. And it was this massive creature that looked like a pumpkin tree and I was so completely in awe of her. Plus, she was this fearsomely amazing engine designer and— Sorry, what were we talking about? Oh, yeah. Picking names. Right, hit me with it.'

The pause was disconcerting. She just sat there, staring at me.

'Well, er… You look a bit like…' I caught myself before I finished that sentence. *Oh, crap. Lem, you idiot. You can't tell a woman she looks like a horse! No matter how much she* actually *does.* 'You remind me of a species from my planet. They're really majestic and beautiful, but also incredibly powerful.'

Nice save there. Spock flopped her head onto the floor and went to sleep.

My new friend touched her hoof to her heart – well, where her heart might be. 'Aw, thank you. That's so sweet.'

'When I was a kid, we went to go' – *do not say riding* – 'meet them in a place called Bexley. That's it. I'll call you Bexley. What do you think? Is that okay?' I clenched my fists on the floor, hoping I hadn't put my foot in my mouth. I needed this encounter to go better than the whole horse-riding thing had gone – my one and only encounter with horses led to an afternoon in the urgent care centre at Queen Elizabeth Hospital in Woolwich.

She nickered. Genuinely nickered. 'Well, when you say whatever name it is you're saying, I just hear my name. So, yeah. Works for me. But that's a really lovely story. Thank you for explaining – I am so honoured. That might be the nicest story anyone's ever told me.' I looked down at my watch and, sure enough, displayed on the face were the words: BEXLEY SPEAKING.

She reached out a hoof and touched the window in front

of her. I got the sense she might be a hugger – but we still had the prison walls between us.

There was a moment's silence, interrupted – at least on my side – by a noisy fart from Spock. She lifted her head up and looked around. 'Rude,' she declared, then flopped back down onto the floor.

I scratched my head frantically. 'There's so much I need to ask. Where do I even begin?' I pressed my fingers into my temples and tried to herd my thoughts into some kind of order. 'Why were we imprisoned? How can there be an inter-planetary arrest warrant for a dog? Where are we being taken? What will happen to us? How am I going to get home? When's lunch? You probably don't have any answers, but...' My shoulders fell as I exhaled.

The wall at the front of the cell beside Bexley's turned transparent at the same time as Holly announced, 'The pris-oner in cell C is requesting permission to communicate with you. Shall I put her through or decline the call?'

It was harder to see into the cell in question because it was at a ninety-degree angle to mine. It looked like it contained ... maybe a rubbish bin? Too hard to tell in the dark. But I didn't see anything that looked like a person. 'Yeah, sure, Holly. But where is she? I don't see anyone.'

Bexley strained forwards, putting her – er – muzzle against the surface of the window. She used one hoof to wipe away the fog her breath created. 'Oh my gosh, you're a lonely robot! I've heard of you, but I've never met one. What an incredible experience this is turning out to be. Except for all the kidnapping, and interrogation, and being held against our will, obviously. I mean, that's a pretty big downside, so I don't want to declare it a total win. But, um, yeah. It's so nice to meet you.'

'Hey, meatsacks,' said a voice that somehow smelt like

money. PRISONER IN CELL C SPEAKING, according to my watch.

'Hiya. Welcome to the prison gang,' I said to the hoover in the window.

'I think I might have answers for some of your questions – even if they are really quite tedious.' The voice sounded like it belonged to someone who lived in a warehouse conversion in Shoreditch. The kind of person who would own both an Aga and a Saluki named Figgy – or possibly Gustav. 'For starters, we're aboard a bollarding bunnyboo ship. Our captors are bounty hunters, who intend to turn us in to the galactic authorities in order for us to stand trial for our alleged crimes and, more importantly – at least in their tiny frolicking minds – for them to be paid the cracking bounty on each of us.'

Several of those words made no sense in the context of the sentences, but I forced myself to stay with the bigger picture. Which is why I shrieked, 'What? That can't be! I haven't committed any crimes. How can there be a space-bounty on me? I've never even left Earth.'

Bexley's ears stood straight up. 'No, that … that's impossible … I would never. I don't even run faster than the posted speed limit. And I never deviate from—' She stamped a hand-hoof on the floor. 'And I certainly wouldn't steal a… No, that's not … it isn't—'

A cord extended from the cylindrical object in cell C. 'Relax, cream puffs. You didn't let me finish. They've taken us all in the hope of collecting the bounty on us – but the flickers are incompetent. They don't know what the cup they're doing.' A sucker cup emerged from the end of the cord and suctioned itself to the window. It slid around the surface in no pattern that was apparent to me. 'And you're here, sandwich, because Spock is here. She's been accused of some bookshelf or other and you're her responsible adult.'

The light in the hub area between our cells sprang to life and, a split second later, the window-wall opacified.

'The prisoner's left hand will step forwards to attend questioning.'

I hauled myself to my feet. For the first time since I'd woken up on this spaceship – if I believed what everyone kept telling me – it dawned on me that I had no shoes. It had been cold in the cottage in Algonquin Park, so I'd bundled myself up in a hoodie, T-shirt, brushed cotton pyjama bottoms, and mismatched socks. But no shoes.

A small door appeared again, as it had before. Green bunnyboo walked in, followed by Blue. Green held the same projectile weapon she had used before, pointed at me.

'The prisoner's chaperone will attend questioning now.'

I didn't need to look at my watch to know it was Blue who was speaking. I could see her mouth moving. The same rope lead the bunnyboos had used on Spock earlier dangled from her paw as she took a step towards me, her other paw outstretched. She reached up and then seemed to realise she couldn't reach my neck. She made a half-hearted attempt to jump and throw the lead over my head. Spock moved to position herself between me and the bunnyboos.

Blue had the decency to look sheepish. 'Er, do you mind?'

I held up a paw – no, that was ridiculous, I had hands. I

may have fallen down a rabbit hole but I was still a perfectly ordinary human with hands and feet and shame. I held my hands in front of myself in an attempt to reboot the conversation. 'There's been a mistake. Whoever you think Spock is, I promise you she isn't. You want to get your bounty, right? And you want justice to be done.' Surely they could be reasoned with?

Blue put her paws on her hips. Her long, velvety soft ears flooped floopily. She lifted both paws and motioned for me to put my head in the lead. 'Come on, just … please. We can talk about this, but we have to follow the proper procedures.'

I put my own hands on my hips, like some sort of time-delayed mirror. Well, a stretchy circus mirror. Whatever. 'Look, I'm not coming with you until I get—'

Green stepped forwards, pointing the same gadget she had shot me with earlier at my stomach. Instinctively, I raised my hands – just like people do in cop shows on the telly.

'We don't answer your questions,' Green said. 'Let Blue put the lead on you, or I'll take you to the interrogation room in a bucket.'

'Fine, all right, I'll come with you. Just leave Spock alone.'

Blue hoisted the rope lead up, trying to toss it over my head, like someone trying to lasso a giraffe.

'You don't need that. I promise, I'll come with you,' I said.

Green lifted her weapon towards me again. 'Just put the lead on your own head, you furless giant. The sooner you cooperate, the sooner this will all be over.'

I picked up the lasso end of the lead and slipped it over my head, never taking my eyes off Blue. 'This is all a huge misunderstanding. You'll see. I don't know what you think Spock did but, where I come from, dogs can't be charged with crimes.'

Blue sighed. 'There, there. Good oaf, now let's go. You'll be back to your master soon enough.'

'What? My what?' But Blue yanked on the other end and led me from the room. I had to bend at the waist to get through the tiny cell door. The surprisingly strong creature was pulling on the lead, so I bonked my head on the frame.

The central area outside the room was brightly lit. The four other cells were opaque. From this side, I could see the faint outlines of the doors for walking through as well as the smaller ones for food.

Blue wasn't overly harsh with the lead – I had worried she was going to drag me down the corridors, but that didn't seem to be the case. She just led me along, pointing me into a small room that turned out to be a lift. Green followed us in. There were no buttons – I couldn't see how it was controlled.

When the lift moved, I became acutely, internally aware of ... something. Some key difference. When a lift moves, you can generally feel whether it's going up or down. Not so on the ship. It felt like we were floating – except no one's feet left the floor.

Maybe this really was space— *No. I'm not buying into that without proof.*

After a few nauseating moments, the lift door whooshed open. Green stepped out first. Blue pointed an adorably dainty little paw to the left and motioned for me to move. A few metres down the hall, they both stopped. On my left, a door slid open.

They led me into what looked like a corporate meeting room. Except in miniature. Like a tastefully appointed board-room for dignified six-year-olds. Blue selected a chair and sat down. Her little cotton-puff tail poked through a hole in the back that seemed designed for that very purpose. She gestured for me to take a tiny seat across from her.

I looked down at the round table – the surface of which came up to my knees. The chair's seat was on a level with my calves. 'Er, really?'

Green, still standing by the door, took a step forwards and raised her weapon. I suppose it was meant to be a menacing sort of move, but it was like being threatened by a teddy bear. *A teddy bear with a gun*, I reminded myself. Some sort of tranq gun, at least. And who knew if it had other settings?

I lowered myself into the toy chair as carefully as I could. My knees, obviously, wouldn't fit under the table, instead butting up against it at nearly chin height. I tried sitting with my legs akimbo – one knee to either side of me – but that wasn't nearly as comfortable as it sounds. I shifted, putting my legs to one side, then tried to pivot my torso to face Blue.

'Thank you.' Blue nodded her head and clicked a button on the device in her paws. 'For the purpose of the recording, please state your name, species, and full genome sequence.'

I caught myself mid-giggle. 'My, er, okay... My name is Leighton Ellis McMaster. People call me Lem. I'm from Earth. Er, that is, I'm a human. And I have no clue what my genome sequence is.'

Leaning back in the chair, Blue said, 'Please confirm whether you agree you are the left hand for the entity known as Spock, also from Earth. Species Canis familiaris.' She made a sort of adorable little sneer. 'Genome sequence also unknown.'

I shifted my arse to try to get a bit less uncomfortable in the toy chair. 'I don't know what a left hand is. Well, no. I mean...' I raised a hand – then realised it was the wrong one. Lowering it, I waved my actual left hand around helplessly. 'But, er, I am her responsible adult, if that's what you mean.'

Blue looked at the screen again. Her little button nose

wrinkled, making her whiskers shiver. 'Please state for the record the nature of your relationship to Spock.'

'The nature … my relation — What?'

Blue blinked those ridiculous cartoon eyes and repeated herself. 'Please state for the record the nature of your relationship to Spock.'

'She's my dog.'

Blue turned to Green and said something I couldn't hear. I hopped around on my stupid, tiny seat to face Green. I could see her mouth moving in response, but again, my watch didn't deign to translate it. I shifted awkwardly in the little chair so I was facing Blue again. 'My translator doesn't know what to make of that,' she said. 'Please clarify. We need to document your relationship to Spock. Is she your lover? Your child? Your nibling? The [no frame of reference] of your [no frame of reference]?'

'The what of my what? No, she's my dog. I … er … that is … I own her.'

Blue's face was overcome by what looked to me like abject horror. Her jaw fell slack and she gawped at me, open-mouthed, for several seconds. 'You claim ownership over a sentient being? Like, she's your slave?' She faced Green again and spoke rapidly but silently, gesticulating wildly. Looking at me again, Blue said, 'So … you … believe that the sentient being in your care is … a possession … not worthy of rights in her own self?'

I bit back a startled laugh. 'What? Well, no … that is … I mean … she has rights. She has volition. But she can't be held legally responsible for her actions. She's not sentient… No, that's not… I mean, she's sentient in the classical sense. She has feelings, obviously. She has senses. What I'm trying to say is she isn't sapient.' I scratched my head. 'Yeah, that's what I'm getting at – she lacks sapience.'

Blue furrowed her fuzzy little brow. 'She … lacks … wisdom?' She placed her paws on the surface of the table. 'Yet you – a being who regards a plainly sentient creature as a mere possession – think you are wise? Is that what you're telling me?' Her little whiskers jiggled jauntily. 'Really?'

'Well, I—' And then I faltered. Because I didn't really have an answer to that question. I tried to lean back in my little chair but succeeded only in tipping it over. I fumbled to recoup the remains of my dignity.

Just as I righted the chair, a purple light flashed somewhere. The bunnyboos spoke rapidly to one another silently. 'Something urgent? Do you need to —'

Green stabbed me in the bum with her weapon. 'Shut up!'

Geez. 'Okay, all right. What do I need to do?'

The bunnyboos carried on their harried conversation. After a moment, Blue ran-waddled out of the room. Green pointed her weapon at me and said, 'Back to your cell. Quick, quick, hop!' She poked me in the belly with the weapon as she picked up the end of my lead.

We headed back into the corridor. Green was a lot harsher with the lead than Blue had been.

'D'you mind? You're giving me rope burn.'

She grunted as she kicked me in the arse, forcing me into the lift. This time, I saw the creature speaking to activate the lift – well, I assumed that was how she operated it. For all I knew, she was on the phone with her mother. Or ordering a pizza.

When the lift doors slid open on the prison cell level, Green shoved me out. 'Come on, pervert. Get a move on. Back to your cell with your treasured possession.' She galloped – in so far as a bunny can be said to gallop – down the hall, dragging me behind her.

She kicked me a final time, pushing me through the little door into my cell. Spock ran to greet me, practically knocking me down as I scrambled to get upright. She covered me with kisses.

'Lem back,' she squealed, wagging her tail so hard I thought she'd knock herself over. She danced around. 'Spock worry. Spock lonely.'

'I got you, mate. I'm okay.' I ran my fingers through her fur.

She leant against me, then wagged her tail once more. 'Give dinner.'

The food tray had been pushed into the room while I was gone. Without opposable thumbs, Spock hadn't been able to open the dishes – which was lucky for me or she'd have eaten both our lunches.

I picked the tray up and carried it to the little table. I'd previously thought of it as an end table – but given what I'd seen in the conference-cum-interrogation room, it was probably meant to serve as a dining table. 'Holly, which of these is which, please?' Somehow, I couldn't stop myself from looking at my watch each time I addressed the AI.

'From your current perspective, the one on the left is Spock's.'

'Thanks.' I peeled the lid off the indicated dish. It appeared to be the same beige porridge, but I gave it a sniff. 'Is that…?'

'Sweet potato vindaloo,' said Holly.

I set it down next to the ocean of drool on the floor under Spock's face. 'Here you go, mate. Bon appétit.' She gulped half of it down in the first bite as I returned to investigate what had been set out for me.

'For your own meal, you have another two items your mind flagged as favourites: avo on toast and Bakewell tart.'

I picked up the dish and peeled back the lid to reveal the bland-looking sludge. 'Where's the other one?'

'It's avo on toast and Bakewell tart,' Holly repeated. 'They are favourites of yours, are they not?'

I groaned. 'Should have known better.' My stomach emitted a loud grumble, so I tucked in. The bizarre combination of textures and flavours was almost enough to put me off my food – but I was too hungry to be picky.

Once I'd eaten, I asked Holly to contact Bexley. 'Oh, and er… Can you designate the prisoner in cell C "Henry", please? And can you see if she's available as well? Oh, and switch the lights off, please?'

As the room dipped into darkness, the window-wall faded into transparency again. Both my new friends' cells were opaque, but the other two cells were clear. One was empty. But the prisoner in cell D – between Bexley and Henry – was obviously the big yellow bird I'd accidentally woken up earlier in the – well, the coffin-fridge room. The one that looked like a dentist's office.

As soon as they spotted me, the bird-creature stood to her full height, spread her wings, and puffed out her feathers. Although I couldn't hear anything, it looked like she was doing a pretty good squawk too.

It was hard to judge relative heights across the space, but even with her crest up, she still looked to be shorter than most humans. She had two little taloned hands stemming out from her shoulders, just at the tops of her wings.

'There's no answer from either Henry or Bexley at this time, Lem,' said Holly.

Spock ran to the window and barked at the spectacle.

'Noisy fluffy friend,' shouted my dog in my dead dad's voice via my watch. 'Hello, feather friend.' She danced in circles, shouting her greetings.

The bird stopped screaming and began to preen itself, chewing its chest feathers in jerky, rapid motions.

After a moment, Holly said, 'The prisoner in cell D is requesting to communicate. Shall I put her through?'

So, it was a she – and presumably a person. 'Yes, please, Holly. And, er, just go ahead and designate her BB.' *May as well run with the big bird thing,* I figured.

The bird-person raised their wings a few centimetres. 'Hello, hi, lovely to meet you. Apologies for my, um – well, you certainly gave me a start. My word, you are strange-looking.' She used both her beak and her fingers to smooth the feathers on her chest and shoulders. 'Sorry, I bet you get that a lot. You're not an actual criminal, are you? Actually, it's just occurred to me, you probably can't speak. I'm sitting here talking to an ent – more fool me.'

'Lem good,' said Spock, sounding offended that anyone would dare to question my honour.

I laughed and patted Spock's head. 'I promise I'm not a criminal. I'm not even the one accused – Spock is. But she's not a criminal either. It's all just a misunderstanding.'

Spock forced her head into my hand. 'Rub cheeks.'

BB puffed up her feathers again, before lowering herself to sit on the floor. At least, I assumed she was sitting – it was too dark to see how she'd arranged herself, only that she'd dropped closer to the ground.

'And you're sure you're sentient?' With a little clawed hand, she stroked her beak.

'Yeah, I'm sentient, I promise. My name's Lem. And this is my dog, Spock.'

She tapped her beak with a single talon. 'Yes, I met your spouse earlier.'

'My sp—' My words were cut off by the appearance of Henry in her cell.

'Henry is requesting permission to—'

'Yeah, Holly. Patch her in,' I said. 'And can you try Bexley again, too, please?'

'Yo, ugly bags of foetid water,' came the gender-neutral voice of the trucker with a pot of gold that belonged to my new friend, Henry, the featureless cylinder with an attitude. 'What took you flanging cretins so long?'

HENRY SPEAKING declared my watch face – rather unnecessarily, I thought.

'Pardon?' said BB and I in unison.

'Cat's away, so it's time for the mice to play,' said Henry. 'What the corncob are we waiting for?' Two hoses extended from her body and waved around until she appeared to be hugging herself.

BB clucked wordlessly. 'I'm sorry, I beg your pardon my good robot, but what exactly do you mean?'

A limb of some sort extended from Henry's cylindrical shape before retracting back into it. 'I mean, you feathery windbag, that the flanking bunnyboos have left the ship. We're on our own. Now, what are we going to do about it?'

BB began preening her feathers again. I recalled reading somewhere that parrots sometimes did that as a coping mechanism for anxiety. 'Well, what can we do from inside these dreadful prison cells?'

Bexley's cell popped into view as her lights went out. 'Oh gosh. Hey, everyone. I'm so sorry I missed the start of the party. I hope you didn't have all the fun without me. It was time for my daily urination and it can take a quarter of an hour when it really gets flowing and – oh my gosh, I'm doing it again, aren't I? I'm so sorry. I have a habit of oversharing when I'm nervous and obviously if any—' Her massive lower jaw fell slack and she nickered anxiously. 'Oh my gosh, you're so beautiful.' This last bit seemed to be addressed to BB, who clucked in response.

'Look, if you meatbags want to stay in your cells,' said Henry. 'You're welcome to do so. But I thought we might make a bit of mischief while we're here. Who's with me?' Something flickered and the window-wall seemed to become less … substantial in a way I couldn't quite describe. I reached out to touch its surface – and my hand went straight through!

5 / ESCAPE

'Er,' I said.

'Well,' said BB.

Bexley nickered. 'Oh, that's unexpected.'

'Outside!' Spock leapt through the was-window and into the open space beyond – before running back to collect her treasured brain.

Henry didn't say anything; she just rolled forwards, wobbling a bit as she crossed the lip of the formerly solid wall. The open space in front of the cells lit up as she did so.

I sneezed three times in quick succession.

'Um, Henry.' Bexley's pointed ears swivelled like little satellite dishes and she ran a hoof down the length of her mane. 'I don't want to sound ungrateful or whatever, but what just happened?' With the lights on, I saw her – well, all of them – more clearly for the first time. Bexley still resembled a horse with boobs – she stood on her hind legs, though. Tiny, too – the top of her head only reached my shoulder. She was covered in soft chestnut-coloured fur but her mane and tail were fairer – more of a golden blond. Her eyes sparkled with an array of different colours.

Henry looked every bit as industrial-cleaning-appliance-esque as she had when she was a silhouette. 'I told you cheese curds. The bunting bunnyboos were called away. They're gone. They took the guacamole shuttle and —' She extended a hose and whooshed it away from her blue cylindrical body.

Guacamole? Bunting? What?

BB shook her head, fluffing out her feathers. 'Now, um, my robotic friend... What is happening here?' Her brightly coloured wings raised and lowered. Aside from a small patch of bare skin on her cheeks, she was covered entirely in feathers. Most of them were a vivid gold, but some on her wings and crest were a whole rainbow: green, turquoise, royal blue, red, and orange.

Henry roll-danced in circles around the space between the prison cells, Spock nipping playfully at her wheels. 'Easy-peasy, lemon-squeazey, mozza balls. I hacked the [no frame of reference] and reprogrammed it to [no frame of reference] using the [no frame of reference]. Simples! Even you suet pellets could do it.' What appeared to be a dough-hook emerged from her cylindrical body, turned a few circles, and then disappeared back into her. 'Well, maybe not.'

Bexley raised her head and sniffed the air, nostrils flaring. 'Well, then. I don't know about the rest of you, but I vote we go exploring. Based on what little I've seen of the ship, I'm guessing it's a Firefly class. Maybe a series fourteen or a thirteen. You can tell by the shape of the [no frame of reference]. Those are a dead giveaway.' She tapped her hand-hoof on a nearby wall a few times. 'Yeah, I think it's got to be the series fourteen. We must be on one of the middle levels. Those are entirely configurable to the customer's needs. And if that's the case...' She let her voice trail off as she left the prison area.

With a shrug, I set out after her – Spock on my heels. No way was I going to stick around there after I had been locked up for so long. I figured, maybe, if I stuck with Bexley, we could get some answers and find a way out of there. 'No clue what she's saying, but she certainly sounds like she knows what she's talking about,' I muttered. 'Hey, Bexley, wait up!'

We passed the lift where the bunnyboos had taken me on the way to the interrogation room. Bexley's long blond mane flowed gracefully behind her as she ran. She opened a door and headed in. I ducked and followed her through, scratching my arm absent-mindedly.

It was a small room full of ... stuff. Equipment-type stuff. Bexley gambolled through the space, touching cabinets and machines. 'Oh gosh, yes. This is definitely the series fourteen. See the layout of the fittings here?' She pointed to a nondescript device that could have been a router or a hard drive or, well, pretty much anything. 'On the thirteen, the configuration would be reversed.'

She turned and trotted back out of the room – almost colliding with Henry and BB. 'I'm going to go investigate the engine room. Did you know the [no frame of reference] has ... well, anyways, whatever. You don't want to listen to me banging on about the ship's specs or we'll be here all day.' She waved her hooves in front of her chest. 'Oh, and the kitchen will be down there. I don't know about you lot, but I'm absolutely famished.'

Her words trailed off as she pranced down the hallways and climbed into a small room. I followed her in, expecting it to be another lift, but it was a ladder. She was climbing down.

I was about to join her when I remembered. 'Spock can't do ladders. I guess I'll see you down there, Bexley.'

She looked back up without stopping. 'Sure. Bottom level.'

BB followed her into the ladder tube. Henry rolled up to me and said, 'Ladders are the work of the devil.'

I sneezed again and sniffled as it struck me: how was Bexley climbing? She had hooves? How did that work? I shook my head.

The three of us – Henry, Spock, and me – crammed into the lift. Once again, I had the strange sensation of motion but without directionality. Definitely had a bit of a cold coming on – I felt the pressure in my sinuses as we moved. We emerged a few moments later – just as BB was climbing out of the stairwell.

'I'm going to go investigate the engine room,' said Bexley. 'I'm so excited – I've never been on a series fourteen before. Not a finished one, I mean. If you two go through that door' – she punched a hoof to her left – 'you should find the kitchens. Do you want to check out what supplies are available?'

She headed in the other direction, Henry rolling after her.

BB stood slightly higher than my navel. She fluttered her wings, exposing the long blue and green feathers beneath. 'Well, I guess all we're good for is kitchen duty.' She rocked side to side, shifting her weight from one clawed foot to the other. 'It's not like I went to medical school or anything. I'm a doctor, not a cook.' She walked up to the door, which slid open. 'Still, well, best do as the bossy one indicated.'

For the most part, the room looked like a small, but perfectly serviceable, industrial kitchen – though there were a few appliances I didn't recognise. BB turned her attention to cupboards, rifling through the contents.

'Dinner time?' asked Spock with a swishy wag of her tail.

I spotted something that made my breath catch in my throat. 'Er, BB, I think we might have a problem.'

She set down a packet of something and turned to face me. 'What is— Oh!'

In the far corner of the room, there was a glass-fronted

walk-in fridge. It was filled with smoke. 'Oh my days! I think the fridge is on fire,' I shouted. I leant close to the door, cupping my hands around my face to get a better view.

BB ran towards me, fluttering her wings. Even with her crest up, she was still only as tall as my shoulders. She hissed at me. The translator didn't say anything, but her meaning was clear enough. 'That, you bald monkey, is a person. And, for the record, most species consider it incredibly rude to discriminate against fluidics and/or other gestalt entities.'

I felt my face flush. BB turned towards the fridge, raising her wings up. 'Hello. Are you okay? That is, obviously, you're not okay – you're in a fridge. I do hope you're not hiding from us. We're perfectly lovely people, I promise. Well, I certainly am – and I'm happy to vouch for my new friend, the quadruped.' She extended a wing in Spock's direction then glanced briefly at me. 'Though I'll confess, I'm not one hundred per cent convinced about the naked hatchling here.'

Glaring at BB, I shook my head. 'I'm not a hatchling.' Turning to the fridge, I added, 'I'm sorry for my rudeness. It's my first time away from my planet. I've never met a, er, gestalt entity before. It's lovely to meet you. My name's Lem. And this is my dog, Spock.' Spock ran up beside me and put her head in my hand as I spoke.

The voice that replied sounded like butter. Like butter would sound if butter made a noise. Well, a noise other than the splat of toast falling buttered side down. Smooth, creamy, rich. 'Oh my! An introducer – how quaint. And greetings, fellow sentients. That is, I take your word for it that you are a person.'

There was an awkward pause before BB reached out to open the fridge. 'May I? I promise you'll come to no harm.'

'Yes, of course. Absolutely.' The voice from my watch

was incredible – like if Amy Winehouse spoke the way she sang. 'I'm sorry to appear ungracious. When I was alerted to the fact the prisoners had escaped their cells, I am ashamed to admit, I feared the worst. The bunnyboos had led me to believe you all a group of dangerous, ravenous killers.'

BB cranked the handle and pulled the fridge door open. Her pupils contracted and dilated. 'Oh, we're not that.'

I hadn't imagined it; what floated out was smoke. Well, like if a smoky rainbow explosion in a glitter factory tripped and fell into an oil slick. She hovered gracefully in the air, moving closer to BB without appearing to change position. It almost looked like she was hiding behind BB.

'We should go and find the others,' I said. 'Tell them we found someone.' I twisted my torso to scratch at my back. *Why am I so itchy?*

Her head bobbing as she danced from foot to foot, BB said, 'Yes, actually that's a good idea. Communicator, please ask Bexley and Henry to join us in the—' She clucked her beak. 'Is there a lounge or a dining area nearby? Somewhere we can sit and talk?'

'Oh, that is an excellent suggestion, BB. Yes, the dining lounge is just through there.' The entity's body formed a gassy limb, pointing to a closed door. 'I'll put together a selection of beverages and nibbles. As the ship's cook, I have all your profiles saved. I'll prepare something to everyone's liking.'

'Good idea,' said BB. 'Communicator, ask them to meet us in the dining lounge. Given Bexley's familiarity with the ship design, I'm sure she can find it.'

I was glad the glittery one had suggested drinks. My throat felt a bit raw.

'Er, excuse me,' I said to the gaseous entity. 'Do you need, like, a hand or anything? You know, with the preparations.' I scratched my head.

'Oh, you're a darling. Thank you, that would be lovely. If you'd grab some utensils from that drawer over there and a few little plates from that cupboard there.' She indicated both spots the same way, by extending her body in the indicated direction. 'Excellent, thank you. Carry them through to the lounge, please. I'll join you in just a moment.'

I looked in the drawer. 'Sorry, I've got some forks and knives and – I'm not sure, maybe chopsticks – but there is no spoon.'

'Oh, dear me. Yes, of course. They're in the dishwasher. I'll bring them through with the refreshments.'

I still wasn't sure how the entity was going to carry stuff, but I headed into the lounge with Spock.

The door whooshed open as I approached and I ducked into the dining lounge. The setup looked designed to suit about half a dozen people of bunnyboo size. There were a couple of sofas at one end of the room, overlooking a window into outer space. Dropping the plates and cutlery unceremoniously on the nearest table, I made my way to the window. I peered out to the darkness beyond.

We really are in outer space. Everything I'd ever known was gone. The blackness outside the window was unrecognisable. Pinpricks of stars spangled it in an unfamiliar pattern. And nary a planet in sight.

How far from home are we? I was caught in a giant tangle of emotions. Fear Excitement. Awe. And a total discombobulation at the scope of it all. I stood there for a moment, taking in the vastness.

Spock leant against my leg and rubbed her face with my hand. 'Go home now?'

I obliged her by stroking her thick fur. 'Sorry, mate. Not

yet. Truth is, I don't know where home is. Or even when. How long were we in that box before we woke up?'

At the edge of the left-hand side of the window, I could see ... something. 'I'm not an expert on this stuff, you know. I can never even keep astronomy and astrology straight. Is that ... a galaxy? A nebula? A constellation? An aurora? A comet? I just don't know.'

'I don't have the data you're seeking, I'm afraid,' replied Holly – even though I had actually been talking to myself. 'From my data banks, it does appear to be a nebula. The *OED* defines a nebula as a luminous patch made by a cluster of distant stars or by gaseous or stellar—'

'Yeah, all right, thanks. I wasn't actually looking for an astrology lesson.' I pursed my lips as a thought struck me. 'Hey, Holly, can you designate the gassy one Aurora for me, please?'

'Done.'

'Oh my gosh.' Bexley walked through a door I hadn't even noticed. 'Is that where we are? It's so beautiful.' Bexley loped across the room to join me at the window. With one hoof-hand, she stroked Spock's fur in an absent-minded way as we gazed out the window. 'I never get tired of looking into space.'

I sneezed six times in rapid succession.

Bexley looked at me. 'Sorry, I don't know your species very well. And my AI isn't translating whatever you just said. Would you mind repeating it – maybe a bit slower this time?'

I clutched my chest. My throat was trying to seal itself shut. 'Can't ... breathe.'

Spock began weaving between my legs frantically. 'Be okay, Lem.'

Henry rolled into the room. 'What's up, animatronic ham sandwiches?'

Bexley leant in close and sniffed at my face. I sneezed a few more times as she said, 'I don't think Lem is functioning properly. Something seems to have gone wrong with her breathing.'

It's funny but – even as the edges of the room began to dim and blur – all I could think was how grateful I was that she got my pronouns right. Most people didn't – or at least they struggled to understand why an agender person who'd been assigned male at birth would use she and her.

It was a pretty stupid thing to focus on when my ability to think coherently was fading as rapidly as my vision was. But it's what happened.

Spock shouted from some distance away, 'Doctor bird help.' Then I collided with the floor.

———

I awoke with BB leaning over me. There was an oddly shaped oxygen mask on my face. 'She seems to be coming around now, though these readings are meaningless to me. I'm a doctor, not a veterinarian. I've no idea what normal would look like for such a bizarre species. For all I know, that little performance was a mating ritual.'

I was breathing more easily now – a bit – but I felt like I was on fire. I fought to refrain from scratching, otherwise I'd claw right through my skin until it hung off me in tattered shreds. I'd done it before. 'Corticosteroids,' I croaked.

Aurora hovered behind and to one side. Spock was sitting next to – or possibly inside – her, watching everything.

BB bobbed her head up and down. 'You want me to halt your immune system? That doesn't sound right. Why would I do that?'

I fumbled in my hoodie's pocket, pulling out the phone I'd

mostly ignored since I first woke up in this strange place. A few quick clicks and I found the health app with its list of my medications, allergies, and medical conditions.

I handed the device to BB, who stared at it. 'Yes, that's a very pretty picture, Lem. Well done. But what I need is information that will help me understand what's going on with your body.'

She clucked her beak and looked away. 'Ordinarily, I wouldn't like to violate your privacy, but as a doctor, I instructed your AI to grant me access to the medical data in your mind. Nothing else, I promise.'

The little talon-hands near her shoulders flexed and folded a few times. 'It contained some of the information about some of the drugs you might need. You had previously read the chemical composition of a variety of medications you sometimes take. I was able to synthesise and administer adrenaline, prednisolone, fexofenadine, and paracetamol. I couldn't be certain what the purpose of some of them were – but the medical data extracted from your mind said you relied on all of them on either a regular or urgent basis, so I took a stab at it.'

'It explains it all right there— oh. You can't read English.' I was exhausted – all I wanted to do was go to sleep. But I was wired, too – like I wanted to run a marathon. Adrenaline will do that to a person.

'I assume that's a language from your home world and you're referring to the little pictographs on your device, but I'm afraid I don't have any way of knowing what it says.'

'Asthma and allergies,' I said between gasps. 'Normally I always have my EpiPen, but because I was kidnapped from my bed, I only have what's in my p— Wait!' I reached into my pocket for the one other thing in there: my rescue inhaler. 'Bollocks! Only one dose left.' I raised it to my lips and—

'Stop her,' shouted Aurora. Quicker than a flash, BB gripped my arm in her surprisingly strong claw. She plucked the puffer from my fingers with her beak.

'Hey, I need that,' I gasped. A coughing fit took over as I struggled to get my breath. My heart was racing.

Spock was on me in an instant. 'Lem sick?' I let my now-empty hand drop onto her head as she gave my face a thorough sniffing.

Aurora floated closer to me. 'Please let BB have the device, Lem. She can analyse the contents using the mass spectrometer to determine the chemical compound so that she can reproduce it for you.'

BB studied the inhaler, clutching it delicately between two talons. 'Is this salbutamol? That was the last drug compound your mind had catalogued as semi-regular. However, you'd never read its chemical makeup, so I was unable to synthesise it. What is it? What is its purpose?'

I held up a finger in what I hoped was a universal 'wait' gesture while I tried to catch my breath. 'Part of my immune system identifies certain things as dangerous and attacks them. I take medicine – antihistamines and corticosteroids – to keep my symptoms under control. But occasionally I have more intense episodes.' I held the mask to my face and breathed as slowly as I could. 'Salbutamol is a ... bronchodilator.'

Aurora tinged a sort of hot pink. 'Your airways spontaneously closed? You mean, your body tried to kill you?'

'So it would seem.' I breathed deeply on the gas pouring in through the mask. 'I think I'm allergic to Bexley.'

I was resting, but not sleeping, curled up in a ball on the short bed, when the door to the medlab slid open. The medlab itself was twin to the prison cell area, though without the dividing walls and with a lot more cupboards and equipment.

'Heya,' said Bexley. She was silhouetted in the doorway about two or three metres away, pawing at the floor with one of her foot-hooves. The bright light of the hallway behind her contrasted with the medical facility's dimness, creating a halo effect. 'I just came by to return Spock's ... um ... whatever this is.' She tossed the brain to Spock, who leapt up to grab it.

'And to see if you were okay, obviously,' Bexley contin-ued. 'I mean, I know you are – BB told me that already. But it was my fault you ... got sick in the first place. And then my fault you got even worse. When you collapsed, I was the one who carried you here. And, if your theory is right that you were rejecting me – I mean that your body was rejecting me – then I definitely made you worse by doing that. But, then, I also saved your life, since no one else could have got you here before you stopped breathing altogether. So…'

I hauled myself up to a sitting position, curling my legs under myself. 'Hi, Bexley. Yeah, I'm sorry. I'm pretty much allergic to everything – it's so embarrassing.'

She swiped a hoof over her head, pushing her forelock down over her face. Shuffling her weight from foot to foot, she said, 'You shouldn't be ashamed of your body – it is what it is. It doesn't make sense to worry about a physical thing you have no control over.' She nickered, sounding awkward.

Spock ran to Bexley. She shoved her face into Bexley's hoof-hand. 'Hello, friend. Got treats?'

Bexley obliged by petting her head. She knelt and nuzzled Spock's face with her own for a few moments. 'No treats, sorry.' Standing back upright, she added, 'BB said to tell you she thinks she can create a drug that will inhibit your immune system so that we can, well, so we can be near one another without me accidentally killing you.'

I blinked. 'Oh, wow! I want to believe. Really, I do. I just … plenty of people have claimed to be able to help. But none ever have. All the meds I've ever found have only managed to ease the symptoms a bit.' As always after an attack, I was shattered. I leant back into the pillows. 'Anyway, tell me what you've found out while I was otherwise engaged.'

Bexley stroked Spock's head, but Spock got up and padded back over to me. She stretched – her front paws on the bed – and sniffed my face thoroughly. She'd already subjected me to several olfactory examinations in the last hour.

'Lem rest.' Having delivered her prescription, she arranged herself into a comfy position on my feet and farted.

Bexley squatted on the floor – in a position most humans

wouldn't find comfortable. 'So, it turns out most of Henry's memory was wiped. Same goes for the ship's data banks. Henry knows how to pilot the ship – and I can keep her flying – but neither of us has any clue where we are. BB's knowledge of space-geography is even less than my own, so she's no help on that front. And our internal communications are fine, but the ansible is down, so we can't call for help.'

Spock lifted my hand with her head, so I ran my fingers through her fur. It helped stave off the panic. How on Earth were we supposed to get home? 'What about Aurora? She works for the bunnyboos – she must know what's going on. And isn't she going to force us all back into our cells?'

Bexley tapped her hoof on the floor in front of her and opened her mouth to reply just as a rainbow cloud appeared from around the corner, guiding a floating tray.

'Hey, Aurora,' said Bexley.

Spock leapt off the bed and wagged her tail. 'Dinner?' She danced in circles around and through Aurora.

Aurora shimmered and vibrated. 'Oh, child, that tickles. Careful or you'll make me drop the food.'

'Give,' demanded Spock.

'Hi, Aurora.' To Spock, I added, 'And you, be nice. Where are your manners?' Spock dropped onto her butt and swished her tail across the floor.

'Hello, Lem. I figured you might be hungry, so I prepared the meal your brain had flagged as a most cherished memory – though, for the life of me, I can't understand why you'd want to eat and drink whilst washing yourself. But far be it from me to criticise your kinks and fetishes.'

'While washing myself?' I repeated. 'What?' My mouth watered as I took in the intoxicating aromas that greeted me when I peeled the lid off the first dish. 'Sweet potato vindaloo – I assume that's for Spock.'

'Yes, she requested it specifically. Yours is based on a meal you ate in the bath.' She vibrated as she spoke.

I set Spock's dish on the floor in front of her. She dove in with gusto. I returned my attention to the second bowl. Removing the lid, I was hit by the gorgeous scent of freshly baked dough with tomato sauce and roasted peppers. 'Pizza. Oh! In Bath – not in *the* bath. It's the name of a city. Oh, that smells divine. Just like the Stables.'

Bexley's eyebrows lifted at the mention of stables. 'Um.'

'Sorry, there's this pub in the centre of Bath. The city of Bath. They do handmade pizza and loads of different ciders and beers. And they have the most incredible brownies – gooey chocolatey heaven.'

'Yes, it's all in there.' Aurora extended a nub of an appendage towards the bowl.

I looked down at the lumpy grey porridge. 'It's … all …' I caught the hint of a cidery odour cutting through the pizza. 'Er, thanks, Aurora. You really don't have to go to so much effort. I would be fine with food that just…' The edges of the glitter cloud that was Aurora began to droop. 'But I'm sure it's wonderful. Thank you.' I picked up the spoon and tucked in.

It tasted like someone had dropped a pizza, a pint of perry, and a brownie smothered in raspberry coulis all into the blender. I forced myself to eat a few spoonfuls as Aurora hovered in front of me.

She quivered. 'Well?'

I smiled politely as I struggled not to gag. Giving two thumbs up, I willed my already abused throat to swallow. 'Very nice,' I croaked.

'Lem no like,' said Spock. The traitor had finished her own meal and was sitting in a half-upside-down position, licking her privates.

There was a noise like a sharp intake of breath. How could a gaseous entity manage that? 'You don't like it? My dear Lem, if you dislike it, why would you say you did? What could you possibly hope to gain from this deception?'

Heat rose in my face. *Thanks a lot, Spock.* 'I don't want to be rude. You went to all the trouble to recreate a meal I enjoyed. It would be churlish of me to insult your efforts or make it seem like I don't appreciate your hard work.'

The rainbow cloud seemed to glow more pink as Aurora's other colours receded. 'But why? It's perfectly possible for you to express gratitude for my efforts and also critique the outputs. The one does not diminish the other.'

Across the room, Bexley again tapped her hoof on the floor in front of where she squatted. 'Yeah, Lem. I gotta say, I'm with Aurora on this one. If you say you like something when you don't, how will anything ever improve? It's like my friend [no frame of reference] always says, "if you don't ask, you don't get." Like, this one time when I wanted to go...' She ran a hoof through her forelock, pulling it down over her face. 'Well, whatever, anyways, the point is, advancement depends upon open and honest communication.'

Aurora's colours shifted more towards the turquoise. 'What can I do to improve your meal next time?'

I could hardly argue with their logic. 'Well, yes, if you put it that way. I suppose that makes sense. You're sure you don't mind?'

She shimmered. 'Of course, Lem.'

I bit my lip and took a breath. 'The thing is, we normally eat things one at a time – not all mixed up together.'

The turquoise morphed into a royal blue. Those colours definitely meant something. 'I shall remember that, Lem. Now, I'll leave you to the rest of your dinner – assuming it's not too awful to bear?'

I smiled awkwardly. 'Thank you. I'll be fine with this.' I couldn't wait to get home to normal, boring, predictable food.

'You're certain?'

'Absolutely,' I lied.

She floated out of the room.

Bexley sniffed the air. 'Oh, I'm sorry, do you want me to go, too? I don't know about your species. Is eating something you need privacy for? My species – the areion – are galaxy-famous for our complete lack of shame. It's hard for me to know what other species consider private activities. Like, there's this one species on [no frame of reference] that considers speaking private – they can't stand to see inside another person. Any orifice *at all*. They pretty much think my whole planet is obscene.'

If I'd had more energy, I'd have properly guffawed at that, but I was still weakened by my earlier attack. I managed a small chortle and waved a hand. 'You're good. I'm happy to have the company. And no, eating is definitely not something humans are shy about.'

'Phew, that's good.' She flicked her head, her long blond waves cascading gracefully over her shoulders.

I grimaced as I ate more of the alcohol-flavoured baby food. But I needed to eat, so I made myself keep going. 'So,' I said between mouthfuls, 'why was Henry's memory wiped? Also, when and by whom? What happened to her?'

'Oh gosh, yeah. So weird. She remembers everything right up to when she powered down for a recharge cycle. But when she booted back up in the *Teapot*'s hold, she'd been … tampered with. So creepy. Who would do that?' Bexley tapped the floor in front of her. 'So, what's the last thing you remember before waking up on this ship?'

I swallowed another mouthful of the world's worst stew and set the bowl down for Spock to lick. 'The last thing?

Let's see. Spock and I were on holiday. We'd gone out into the wilderness north of Toronto for some alone time.' A chuckle escaped my lips. 'Actually, I'd decided to reinvent myself as the kind of person who goes off on adventures. A few months ago, I'd moved to Canada – a different part of the planet – as part of that transformation.' I waved my hands around. 'Wasn't really banking on this big of an adventure, was I? Anyway, after a day of hiking, we had dinner, went for a last little walk, and then settled down to bed.'

Spock looked up from my bowl and wagged her tail. 'Walkies?'

I petted her soft fur. 'Not now, babe. Sorry.' Her ears and tail dropped and she headed into the bathroom. Turning back to Bexley, I continued. 'The next thing I remember is waking up in that ... that ... coffin or box or whatever you call it.'

'The stasis pod.' She tapped her hoof again. *Was that like a nod?* 'Yeah, I tried to ask Spock, before you woke up, but she didn't seem to remember much. Or, more likely, she was just too distracted by what you were going through. But anyways, that's similar to what happened to me. I was out with a few friends. There was this new band we all wanted to see. It was amazing – they rocked so hard. The lead singer is the best. She's so amazing. I swear if I ever met her, I would just lose my – well, whatever. Anyways' – it struck me for the first time that Holly had given Bexley a Canadian accent – 'we fell asleep pretty much as soon as we all had sex and then just like you – boom – I woke up in a stasis pod.'

Spock returned from the bathroom and jumped up onto the bed. She rolled onto her back. 'Rub belly.' I chuckled and obliged.

I let out a big sigh. 'So, you were kidnapped just like me. I bet you can't wait to make it home either. What's the first thing you're going to do when we all finally get there, Bexley?'

'Home?' Bexley furrowed her brow. Almost like she hadn't actually considered escape. 'Oh, I suppose —'

BB strode into the room and lifted her wings. 'Greetings, Bexley, Spock, Lem.' She bobbed her head at each of us in turn. 'Apologies, am I interrupting your conversation?'

I raised my hands. 'No, not at all.'

'Lem and I were just talking about what we were doing before we woke up on board the *Teapot*,' said Bexley.

'We'd love to hear your story, too,' I added.

Bexley tapped her hand-hoof in front of herself. *So, it was like a nod.* 'What were you doing before you woke up here? Maybe if we all swap stories we can figure out why we're here.'

BB shook herself, fluffing her feathers. 'Oh, well, it's an interesting story actually. I'd spent several weeks working on a remote planet, helping the indigenous population in their battle against Bowden's malady. Their understanding of medical science was decades behind my people's and, I don't want to brag, but I am one of the peri's pre-eminent physicians. I specialise in xenobiology. It's how I was able to understand your requirements, Lem. Your biology and anatomy are extraordinary – unlike anything I've seen in all my years of practice. You're a bit like if someone mated a sasquatch with a tamarian. Sort of.'

I shook my head to clear it. 'A what with a what?'

Bexley flared her nostrils. 'Oh, did you set your translator to figurative mode and then forget about it? It can be disorientating for a newbie. If so, the AI will be grabbing the nearest word to what those two species are, even if they're only, like, six per cent similar.'

'Oh right,' I said, feeling exhausted.

BB clicked her beak. 'Anyway, you're lucky I'm so good at what I do. I've analysed the differences in your physiology before, during, and after your attack. Also, the medical data I received contained reference to a drug that had shown some promise in treating allergic asthma.'

'Oh! I read about that.'

'Well, yes,' she replied. 'Where do you think I got the information?'

My shoulders fell. 'No, it's no good, BB. I spoke to my allergist about it. It won't be effective on me.'

BB shook her feathers out. 'Yes, this is why you're lucky you found me. Your species' medical science isn't all there is. There are more things in heaven and earth than are dreamt of in your philosophy, Lem. And I – if I do say so myself – am a genius. I need to work on it a bit more, but I believe I can treat your disease.'

My fingers curled tightly around the brushed cotton of my pyjama bottoms. 'You can cure me?' I enunciated each word carefully.

A small squawk escaped BB's beak. 'Cure you? Good heavens, no. I said I was a genius, so perhaps I misled you. I'm a doctor, not a miracle worker. No, I can't cure you. I believe in science, not magic. Your genetic disorder isn't curable – but I can treat you. Perhaps – with luck – I can build on the work done by the scientists who created the drug contained within your memory banks designed to alle-viate your symptoms to a degree. What I mean is, I hope to make it so you can exist in the same room as Bexley without dying. You'd need to take the drug regularly, though.'

Bexley danced in bouncy circles – like a fairground merry-go-round. 'Oh my gosh, Lem. That's amazing. I really want to hug you right now. Well, if I'm honest, I kinda want to hump you. But I won't because I know the drug doesn't exist yet, and I don't want to kill you, but when it does, get ready for either or both of those things because I will definitely want to. You know, but only with your consent. I'm not gross.'

I grinned wearily. 'That would be amazing, BB, thank you. And, Bexley, I'll definitely take you up on the hug – but not the other. Thank you both for being so wonderful. But seriously, though, shouldn't we be focusing our attentions on trying to prevent ourselves from being recaptured by the bunnyboos when they come back? They probably haven't gone far. That's way more important than me.'

Bexley stood still. 'Oh, we have. Don't worry about that. For starters, Henry transferred control of the ship to us so, if they do find us, the bunnyboos won't be able to get in without a fight. But also, since we don't know where we are, we picked a direction at random and got us moving as fast as possible. Every thirty-three minutes, Henry pulls us back out of warp and picks a new heading at random. Second star from the left, so to speak. At, like, warp seven. The manual says you should only take a Firefly class ship to warp four, but the truth is it can sustain warp seven for a few hours without damaging anything. And it can even do short bursts of warp nine if you know how to talk nicely to it. But you'll kill the flux capacitor if you do that more than a couple of times.'

I blinked as my brain fought to process all the mixed metaphors.

She ran a hoof through her mane. 'Figurative mode strikes again?'

I nodded. 'Takes some getting used to.'

A delicate clawed hand emerged from under one wing – probably around waist height. She patted my face with it, gently running the talons from my forehead to my chin. 'I'll leave you two to talk.' She jabbed one of her lower hands at Bexley. 'Just promise me you won't come any closer than you are now. Those drugs we discussed earlier are far from perfect. No hugging or humping the patient, please.' She stroked Bexley's long nose and left the room.

'I cranked the recyclers up to max just to be sure,' said Bexley. I couldn't tell whether she was talking to me or BB, but I appreciated the gesture.

Spock let out an obstreperous fart. Bexley's nostrils flared again. 'Wow, she does that a lot, eh?'

I reclined into my pillows. 'She does, but you only have to worry when they're quiet. Those are the ones that can clear a room.'

'I'll bear that in mind. Anyways, you seem tired, I should let you get some rest. Besides, I gotta check on those engines again.'

'Good night, Bexley.'

'Good night, you two.'

'Bye friend,' said Spock, before turning three times on the bed and settling in. 'Make dark,' she added. The lights dimmed in response, leaving me to dream of home.

'Is it tomorrow yet?' I finished brushing my teeth with the weird electric implement that Holly had directed me to. It was kind of like an electric toothbrush, but also not. 'Hey, Holly, how long did I sleep? And how many days have I been here?' I'd only booked the hire car and cabin for a few days. If I wasn't back in time, I'd be facing a fortune in late fees.

There was an unusual pause from Holly.

'By shipboard time,' it said eventually, 'it has been one point six three days since you first awoke in the stasis pod.'

I stared at my reflection in the mirror. I'd done a full course of facial electrolysis a few years back, so at least I didn't have to worry about a five o'clock shadow. That would be the last thing I needed – I despised facial hair. On myself, I mean. Bexley's face was entirely covered in soft fur – it looked good on her. But I still hated it on me.

'What do you mean,' I replied, 'by shipboard time? How does that compare to normal time?' I prodded at what might be a pimple coming up on my chin.

'Please restate the question,' said Holly.

'Well, I can't have been here that long.' I stabbed a finger at my reflection in the mirror, unsure of whether it was myself I was arguing with or the fancy chatbot living in my watch. *I'm not sure which option would be worse.* I didn't want Holly's opinion on my sanity. 'My watch ... that is, you haven't even run out of battery.' What if the police got involved? It wasn't exactly like I could tell them I'd been kidnapped by aliens. I'd be locked in whatever Toronto's version of the Maudsley – the psychiatric hospital – was called.

'I arranged for Bexley to upgrade the device while you slept. I can now charge from the air. I believe you'll find she improved my processor speed as well – though that wasn't something I requested.'

I looked at the pyjamas I'd been wearing for however long I'd been here and contemplated putting them on again. I scrunched up my nose. There didn't seem to be any other options. 'Thanks, Holly. Hey, you don't know where I can get some clean clothes around here, do you?'

'Please restate the question.'

'I need clean clothes. These are getting a bit pongy.' I picked up my hoodie and waved it in the air. Even I couldn't stand to be around me.

'That's not a question,' said my infuriating AI.

I shook my head. 'Whatever. I'll ask a real person. But you never answered my last question. How does shipboard time compare to ... well, to Earth time?' With a grimace, I pulled the hoodie over my head.

'Without Earth in my database, I don't have a definitive understanding of timekeeping measures used there. I have estimated a minute based on the beating of your heart – using both the historic data in your device and what's accumulated since you woke up. By my estimation, a ship's day is equivalent to twenty-five hours, forty-two minutes, and eleven seconds.'

I leant back against the sink and pulled my filthy socks on. With no shoes, they not only had to soak up my sweat, but they'd been absorbing everything on the ship's floor. 'And I've been here— What'd you say, a day and a half?'

'One point six four days.'

I headed out of the bathroom into the medlab. 'And how long was I in the stasis pod?'

'Your heart doesn't beat in stasis.'

'My heart doesn't…? Oh, you don't know how long I was in there.' *I'm never going to get my deposit back on the car or the cabin, am I?* I sighed.

After a moment, I said, 'Anyway, Holly, can you set the time on the watch to match shipboard time and show it on the face when no one is speaking, please?'

'Of course,' said Holly.

Spock leapt down off the bed as I emerged back into the medlab's main room. 'Feed Spock?'

'Actually, that's a good idea. Grab your brain and let's go.' It occurred to me I hadn't left the medlab since Bexley carried me here. We stepped out into the corridor. 'Spock, do you know where the kitchen is?'

Her ears folded back. 'No.'

'She hasn't left your side since you collapsed,' said Holly. 'I can guide you to the kitchen if you'd like.'

A few minutes later, the kitchen doors slid open in front of me. Warm, steamy air infused with food scents wafted out. Aurora pulsed and vibrated. Her dominant colour was blue –

but she shifted to more of a yellow hue when she saw me. Assuming *saw* was even the right word...

'Greetings, my corporeal friends. I was just in the midst of preparing food for you and the others. Bearing in mind, of course, your request for a single flavour in your meal.'

'Hello, friend. Feed Spock?'

'Spock! Don't be rude. Good morning, Aurora. Did you, er, sleep well? Assuming you do sleep, that is. Er, do you?' *Of all people, why the hell am I the one dealing with first contact of multiple alien races? I'm probably the worst person on Earth for this task.*

Aurora sort of shimmied over and floated through Spock's face. 'Your breakfast will be ready soon, love. And to answer your question, Lem, I do sleep – after a fashion, though not every day. I slept last week. I'll be good for a few days yet.'

I snuck a peek around the kitchen, hoping there would be something obvious I could help with. 'Is there, er... Is there anything I can do?'

She floated and stretched hither and thither, inspecting various devices. 'Why, I'm sure there are many things you're capable of. But if you mean to assist me with breakfast, I'm just finishing. BB sleeps longer than most corporeals, but Bexley and Henry are in the dining room. I'd suggest sending Spock in first to remind Bexley to stay several metres away from you. Have you had your anti-rejection medications this morning?'

Spock headed into the dining room.

'Yeah, BB left my antihistamines for me. Took them as soon as I woke up.' My eyes darted around the room – I was desperate to spot something that looked like a kettle. 'Say, Aurora, I don't suppose there's any way you could do me some tea, could you? I'm gagging for a cuppa.'

She paused in front of what appeared to be a microwave. The door opened and a bowl seemed to stir itself as she watched. 'Tea? Oh, yes, I have that in your preferences file. I'm afraid, as with everything else, I won't have the actual substance. But I can create something that approximates the flavour. Would you like me to try?'

'Oh, yes, please.' I scratched my head. 'But, er…'

The microwave closed itself and started up again. 'Separate from your food?'

'Please,' I said gratefully. 'If that's okay, I mean.'

'Of course, dear.' She shimmered greenly. 'Now, be a love and let Bexley know breakfast will be through in just a moment.'

'Sure. And thank you.'

As the door to the lounge slid open, I ducked through. The room had been rearranged for social distancing since my last visit the day before. Instead of one big dining table at one end and two sofas set close together at the other, the tables and the sofas had been arranged to face one another. Small dining tables had been set for breakfast in opposite corners. And one of them appeared to be sized for a human.

'Morning, meatsack,' said Henry. It looked for all the world like she was actually using several of her appendages to vacuum the floor and a sofa.

Bexley leapt off one of the sofas and ran in excited circles. 'Hey, Lem! You're awake! I wasn't sure how long your people slept for. Spock seems to sleep more than half the day, so I thought you might be similar. I'm so glad you're here. Henry and I have been discussing what our next move should be. We dropped out of warp overnight, so we need to get us all together to come up with a plan.'

I'd never had people just go ahead and reorganise things to suit my condition. No fuss, no muss. No making a big deal about how inconvenient it was. 'What? Oh, yeah, sure.' I pursed my lips to try to contain the emotions.

Bexley finished her canter and fidgeted on the spot. 'Are you okay? You look like – I mean, I don't know what you look like. I haven't been able to figure out your mannerisms and your face is so weird. I mean, I mean that in the best possible way. I love your face – I just mean I haven't worked out your expressions yet.'

I trod warily to the taller of the tables and carefully pulled out the chair that was obviously meant for me. It felt solid. Someone had welded extra length onto the legs. Everyone else on the ship was closer to Spock's size than mine. 'You made me a new chair? And a table. And you rearranged.'

Bexley flicked her head, sending her long blond waves cascading over her shoulder. 'Well, duh. You couldn't use the furniture that was here – it wasn't sized for you. And as for rearranging… Henry helped with that, didn't you, Henry?'

Henry moved on from the sofa she probably wasn't hoovering. 'Sure. Fine. Whatever.' She nudged me with some sort of spatula-dildo appendage. 'Watch your feet, sandwich.'

I barely had time to raise them before she waved the maybe-vacuum appendage under my chair. Spock was giving her a wide berth. *Maybe Henry really was vacuuming.*

The kitchen door whooshed open and Aurora floated in, steering a cart laden with bowls and mugs. 'I hope everyone's hungry. And, Lem, I've done you the closest I can to your requested beverage.'

Using the same nubby appendage I'd seen her use before, she indicated the bowls and cups for me to take. Then she wheeled her cart over to Bexley.

I put Spock's water bowl down for her, then lifted the lid off one of the breakfast dishes. 'Vindaloo again?'

There was a puddle of drool forming under Spock's face. 'Please? Give Spock.'

'Yeah, all right, mate. Here you go.'

Her tail slapped the air back and forth in furious strokes as I set the bowl down for her. Across the room, Bexley was already deep into her meal. I headed back to the table to investigate what culinary delights awaited me. I lifted the mug to my face with unwarranted trepidation. 'Aaaah,' I sighed what may possibly have been the most contented sigh any human has ever sighed. 'Now, that's a cuppa.'

Strangely, the liquid in the mug had the uncolour and viscosity of water. But the scent was divine – the perfect cup of tea. I lifted it to my lips and took a tentative sip. The temperature, aroma, and flavour profile were exactly right. This was builder's tea ... strong, hot, a splash of oat milk, no sugar.

Except it wasn't.

'How did you manage this, Aurora? It's incredible. I mean, it looks like plain water, but it tastes and smells bang on. It's perfect.'

Breakfast, on the other hand, turned out to be more of the nutrient porridge, flavoured – as per my request – with just one thing. Unfortunately, the one thing was garlic.

———

Once the corporeals – I preferred Aurora's word for us to any of the alternatives Henry came up with – had finished eating, we discussed plans for our next move.

I made myself comfy on one of the sofas, expecting Spock to join me; however, she ran straight to Bexley on the facing sofa a few metres away and curled up on her lap.

'Rub belly,' Spock demanded. Bexley obliged.

'Don't be so rude, Spock,' I said.

Bexley nickered. 'It's never rude to ask for what you want. What a strange society you must come from. Is everyone like you? Do people always have to guess what you desire? How does anyone ever get what they want if they can't tell anyone else what that is?'

I opened my mouth to reply, then closed it. Opened it again. 'Er, I ... that is ... we, well ... what I mean to say is...' I faltered again.

'What she means is that no one gets what they want.' Henry extruded a long thin appendage from her ... er ... lid, twirled it around a bit, and then retracted it. 'But if you cheese curds are finished comparing the bumping arbitrary boundaries of your decking meat-based societies, we do actually have some pressing concerns to deal with.'

'Er... Henry. Can I ask...? Holly seems to have trouble translating some of your words. Is there something I need to do to get it to work properly?'

Henry projected at least half a dozen different appendages, which all twirled or turned or vibrated. 'Flank your uncle, peat moss.'

Bexley folded her lips back, baring all her teeth. 'Henry, it's okay. I'm sure she didn't mean anything by it.'

Aurora turned blue. Yellow glittery effects grew rapidly, until she was mostly yellow, with only a few small blue patches. The blue bits all seemed to face away from Henry.

'My dear, Lem, please remember that you are dealing with different cultures and that other people's experiences may not always align with your own.' Aurora's voice was like auditory velvet.

'I'm sorry. I don't understand. It's clear I said something wrong, but I just...' I could feel a feverish redness spread across my face. 'I want to be certain I understand your meaning.'

Henry sped towards me, appendages still flailing. 'You understand me just fine, you piece of pocking crockery.'

My watch vibrated against my wrist, something it hadn't done since I'd first woken up in this strange new world.

I glanced down at the screen. TEXT FROM BEXLEY: LONELY ROBOTS WERE PROGRAMMED TO NOT SWEAR. IT'S RUDE TO POINT IT OUT.

Oh. 'Er... I'm so sorry, Henry. Please forgive me. I honestly didn't mean to cause offence. I thought my translator was malfunctioning. I'll try to do better.'

She glared at me for a few moments. Or at least it felt like she did – without eyes, it was impossible to know for sure. 'Sure. Fine. Whatever.' One by one, her appendages retracted back into her body. 'Now, can we talk about how we're going to extricate ourselves from this parking pickle we're in?'

I folded my legs up underneath myself on the sofa. 'Okay, so, if I've got this straight, we don't know *where* we are. We don't know *why* they think we're criminals. For instance, Bexley, did they tell you what evidence there was against you?'

Bexley cocked her head to one side – much like Spock did when she didn't understand something. 'No actually. They just told me there was a warrant for my arrest. They said I was wanted in connection with kidnapping a forest on some planet I'd never even heard of. I asked them why they thought that, but they just said it wasn't their job to consider any evidence. "We are not judoon," they said. "Our job is only to deliver the suspects to Trantor for questioning." The bunnyboos recorded everything I had to say, but they didn't actually seem interested in *what* I had to say, only in making sure they recorded it accurately.'

Based on the name Holly had assigned, I assumed the judoon were some sort of space police.

'Yes,' said BB. 'That's similar to my own experience.'

I thought back to my aborted interrogation and flushed. Quickly moving the conversation onwards, I said, 'And, at least in Spock's case, we don't even know *what* the charges are. Nor do we have the first clue where the bunnyboos have gone – never mind when they'll be back. As for why they left—'

Bits of yellow flashed through Aurora. 'Actually, I might be able to shed some light on that last part. I was in the kitchen, preparing lunch for your good selves, when Purple got a call ordering her to Starbug.'

My head jerked an involuntary double-take. 'Starbug?'

Bexley's lips peeled away from her teeth in something vaguely like a smile. 'Figurative mode again?'

I nodded. 'Yeah. Sorry, I assume that's like a shuttlecraft.'

'Yes. Apparently, their compatriots were having a spot of bother at [no frame of reference] so they had to go bail them out,' Aurora said. 'I'm not sure whether they meant that literally or figuratively. However, if everything went to plan, I would have expected them to return by now. Except, of course, we ran away.'

Something had been bothering me since yesterday, but I hadn't been able to put my finger on it because, well, because aliens and allergies and a whole lot of drugs. But it hit me now with glittering clarity.

'Aurora,' I began hesitantly. 'Why are you helping us? How do we know you haven't told the bunnyboos where to find us? With the utmost respect... Why should we trust you?'

Aurora turned yellow. The colours definitely meant something. 'Well, I suppose the short answer is, you shouldn't. Or, at least, you have no reason to do so.' She paused and I had a very strong impression of pursed lips. 'But I will tell you this, a few years ago, I'd got myself into … a spot of bother over some debt. I couldn't see a way out, so I did something I wish I hadn't. But, well … I heard about certain … opportunities' – she paused as if it were too difficult to continue – 'and I signed on as an indentured servant with a group of bunnyboos.'

Bexley leapt up and Henry unfurled something like rabbit ears. 'Indentured,' Bexley cried, 'but that's illegal!'

'Hang on,' I said, scratching my head. 'But the bunnyboos were horrified when they thought Spock was my slave. They called me disgusting.'

Bexley tapped a front hoof as she resumed her seat. *Definitely a sort of nod.* 'Yeah, we call that projection. Whatever you're guilty of, accuse someone else of doing it. Do humans not do that?'

Spock saved me the embarrassment of having to answer that question by emitting a fart so loud, she scared herself awake. She dismounted the sofa she was sharing with Bexley and glared at her with the full force of disapproval that only a dog can manage. 'Rude,' she said.

Bexley nickered and tickled Spock's chin. 'Not me, buddy. Sorry, you did that all by yourself.'

Wearing an indignant expression, Spock walked over and climbed up next to me. 'Rub cheeks,' she said, inserting her face into my hand.

Rolling my eyes, I did as my dog bade. How anyone could think *she* was *my* slave, I'd never understand. 'Sorry, Aurora, I didn't mean to interrupt your story. So you began working for the bunnyboos and—'

'And what?' She glowed a sort of magenta.

I shifted my weight onto my other side. 'Yes, and what?'

'What?'

Henry rolled in circles, extending and retracting implements at random. 'She means, you sparkly windbag, that she wants you to continue your booking story.'

Aurora vibrated and turned a sort of blue. 'Ah, yes, of course. Pardon my ignorance of your human eccentricities. The bunnyboos undertake various jobs – a bit of bounty hunting, a bit of bodyguarding, some courier work, and – well … you get the idea. Anyhow, I have been confined to this ship the entire time, unable to communicate with anyone other than the crew of the ship. I haven't seen any other members of my species or had a non-work conversation for almost four years—'

She broke off, shimmering as her red hues came to the forefront. Bexley jumped off her sofa and cantered to her, running her hand-hooves through Aurora's edges in what I assumed was a comforting gesture.

'If you birches are done,' Henry droned in that overly posh voice. 'We've still got a tanking problem to solve. Which, in case your cupping tears have washed away all semblance of pragma-honking-tism from your tiny meat-based CPUs, is that we don't know where we franking are and we're running out of guttered time.'

With a sharp intake of breath, I almost leapt out of my seat. 'Running out of time? What time? How much time? Are we going to run out of fuel? Life support? Food? What is it?'

Spock sat upright like she was paying attention for the first time since we had finished eating. 'No food?' It still surprised me whenever she interjected into a conversation.

Bexley had finished comforting Aurora and returned to her sofa, safely on the other side of the room from me. 'No, we're okay for food, my beautiful being. It's dilithium crystals that are the issue. When I took us into warp to evade the bunnyboos, I might've-kind've used up our unobtainium. I turned our engines off to conserve the remaining crystals, but we need to find another supply soon. We can only manage a few more minutes at warp. Right now we're just running on, well, desperation and momentum.'

Henry turned in circles again. 'And none of you mince pies ever thought to look at a scabbing galactic map before? My memory banks were wiped by nefarious bunnyboos. What's your excuse, you ignorant blocks of cheese? It never occurred to you to learn about the guacamole universe? You useless sacks of excrement.'

Bexley raised a hoof in objection but didn't say anything.

'Hang on,' I said. 'I've looked at maps...' I flapped my hand, trying to jog something loose. 'Holly can access the data in our heads, right?'

Aurora floated closer and Bexley tapped her hoof. 'Each translator AI has access to its owner's mind's contents, yes.'

I needed to pace to think properly – though I was careful to stay a few paces from Bexley. 'And that includes things we don't consciously remember learning, right?'

Bexley's ears perked up and she leant forwards.

'That is certainly true,' said Aurora. 'But unless one of you has seen a map of this particular region of space, it's unlikely to be of help. Though, I suppose, while I am a mere cook and unlikely to know anything of use, it's possible that one of the rest of you may have some knowledge you don't recall acquiring.'

Bexley rolled her neck. 'Hang on, though. If we can get our AIs to speak to the ship, then there's a chance one of us might have information that connects us to this corner of the galaxy.'

I pivoted on my right foot and swivelled to face the group. 'What if we let all our AIs speak to each other? Then the ship can aggregate and cross-reference all our collective knowledge. We can do, well, I want to say a gap analysis. If we combine what we know, then the ship can build a 3D model of it all. It might be enough for us to fig—'

Bexley leapt up out of her seat and galloped towards me – before stopping herself, skidding on the floor, and backing away. 'Oh my gosh, Lem! That's genius. I'm one hundred per cent serious about that hug. Just as soon as BB's drug is ready. Brace yourself, because you're going to be hugged so hard – actually, I might have to be careful. You look pretty fragile. I'll try not to break any bones. I just really love you!'

Henry extended and retracted a whisk-like appendage. 'I'll admit, it's not the worst bunking idea I've ever heard.'

Bexley sat back down on her sofa – then bounced right out of it again. Henry retracted all her appendages. I could hear Bexley's AI hissing and neighing at her.

Both exclaimed simultaneously, 'A planet!'

'A planet?' I repeated. 'What kind of planet? Do you mean a populated one?'

Bexley cantered in circles around the room on all fours like she couldn't contain her energy. All the excitement woke Spock up and she danced around after Bexley, nipping at her ankles.

The door from the hall slid open and BB walked in, stifling a yawn. 'Morning, all. Oh, what's going on here?'

Aurora floated over and fluttered through BB's uplifted wings. 'Good morning, Doctor. Excellent timing – I believe Henry and Bexley were just about to share some exciting news.'

BB fluffed up her feathers. Her pupils appeared to dilate and contract several times as Aurora floated around her. 'Oh, well, don't let me stop you.'

Bexley pushed her mane over her shoulder and looked at Henry. 'Do you wanna? Or should I? Oh, never mind – I really want to tell them.'

'Far be it from me to—' If Henry had eyes, she would have rolled them at Bexley.

Bexley continued. 'So, last night while you were sleeping — Um, neither Henry nor I need much sleep. So anyways, after we came out of warp to conserve fuel, we set up an alert to ping us if our long-range sensors detected any inhabited planets or space stations or ships or whatever. I mean, we set up *a lot* of alerts.' Henry waved a hose impotently and left the room.

Bexley moved like she was caught in a tug of war between two invisible giants: one pulling her to follow Henry, the other keeping her with us. She tried to rush through the rest of what she was saying. 'Like, there's one if it picks up a big deposit of unobtainium and another for a ship and one for — Anyways, the one that matters right now was the one about M-class planets.'

She galloped out of the room after Henry. She looked back over her shoulder to make sure we were all following as she ran down the hall towards the lifts. 'A few minutes ago, *it pinged!*'

When the lift returned after taking Henry to wherever she'd gone, all five of us – Bexley, Aurora, BB, Spock, and me – squeezed into the tiny lift. 'Command deck, please, computer,' said Bexley, speaking so rapidly I could barely make her words out.

Again, I felt that directionless motion sensation. After a few seconds that felt like hours, the doors whooshed open to reveal a space unlike anything I'd ever seen. A gasp escaped my lips. 'Oh my days.' The window in the lounge area had nothing on this.

This deck was smaller than the others. Ahead of us – and above us – was a large circular space crowned with a clear dome, revealing the universe in all its naked glory. The lift shaft was opaque, so I couldn't see what was on the other side of the deck, but the bridge itself spanned from nine o'clock to three o'clock. Directly ahead of us stood a... *Desk didn't feel like the right word. That made it sound like an office. Bridge stations?* Whatever, it was a sort of table or desk, the entire top of which was a display screen spangled with readouts and images and controls.

Spock dropped her brain and darted straight to the massive curved window. 'Walkies?' She wagged her tail optimistically. I picked up the discarded toy.

Aurora floated alongside her. With only open space behind her, I'd have expected Aurora to disappear, but instead, she *glowed*. Against the window, she was iridescent. 'I've only been allowed on the bridge to clean and always under close scrutiny. I'm with Lem on this one. It's wonderful – I love this space.'

I scanned the horizonless view. 'So, where's this planet then?'

Bexley trotted to the window. Pulling her lips back from her teeth, she chewed on something or nothing for a few seconds before heading to the right-hand bridge station. She tapped a few buttons. 'Sorry, I'm not really a pilot. I can fly, I mean, but I'm a mechanic, so I'm better with the engines than I am with the...' She clicked and swiped a few more times.

Henry rolled up to Bexley's left and plugged a cable into the edge of the table. 'How about this, cheese puffs?' A yellow outline, about twenty centimetres across, appeared on part of the window. 'There's your planet.'

'I don't see anything—' Somehow, I had expected the planet to be visible. Like, it would take up half the window or something, which ... okay ... was naïve.

This time, I knew – I mean, *I knew* – that if Henry had eyes, she would have rolled them at me. Hard. 'Are you some kind of porking moron?'

I looked down at the floor.

Spock put herself between me and Henry. 'Lem good.'

Henry emitted a puff of air through a vent I hadn't spotted before. 'The planet Magrathea is still several offing light-years away. Once we get there, we can find out where in the funk we actually are and hopefully buy ourselves enough unobtainium to get us somewhere useful. If your pal is as good as she says she is, then she'll squeeze every last drop of juice from those lifeless crystals to get us there sometime today. Though I don't see how she can. There isn't enough *voom* in those bollards to get us from here to the kitchen.'

'Magrathea,' I said. 'Like from *Hitchhiker*?' I shook my head. I'd be lucky to get the hang of figurative mode by the time I made it home. But no one was listening to me anyway.

'Hey, you … you inconsiderate person, you,' Bexley said, 'I can make those engines work. There's a lot of things you can call into question and I wouldn't even flare a nostril – but don't you dare question my ability to get engines to … to … to eng!' She stamped a foot-hoof and stormed off the bridge and into the ladder tunnel. It was strange to hear her voice clear as day after she'd left. I was still too accustomed to hearing voices come from people's mouths rather than from my watch. 'I'll get us moving. Don't you fret. You just be ready to steer, pilot.'

'Pilot?' I looked around. 'We have a pilot?'

'No,' said Henry. 'I just sit here because the blinky lights from the pilot's station really bring out the eyes I don't have. You clerking sausage roll, I am a pilot.'

Aurora floated back towards the lift. 'I'll just go put the finishing touches on your breakfast, BB. You must be hungry.'

'Famished, actually.' I'd never really paid attention to how BB walked before. With her huge, clawed feet, she moved like someone in clown shoes. I struggled to contain giggles that would have been entirely inappropriate.

It was just Henry, Spock, and me left. 'So, er,' I began – rather unhelpfully. 'Is there…?'

'Why don't you just sock off, beef jerky?' A stabby-looking appendage emerged from Henry and feinted towards the door. 'Bexley probably needs whatever "help" you think you can provide far more than I do.'

I scrunched up my face. 'How did you manage air quotes there? You don't have hands!'

'Because that's how competent I am, cheese puff,' she replied. 'Donkey girl needs help – undoubtedly more help than you can provide, but if you want to pretend to be useful, go see if you can help her bleed into the engines.'

My eyes went wide. 'She's doing what?'

'I don't know, sandwich. Just go away.'

'Fine,' I said.

While I waited for the lift to return, a host of questions meandered into my brain and congregated. *What was Magrathea like? Could it really hold the key to getting us home? How would we find Earth – didn't all planetary systems basically look the same?*

The lift eventually arrived and Spock wagged her tail. 'See Bexley?' She grabbed the brain from my hand and squeezed past me into the small space.

'Yeah, mate. But I don't know how to find her.' I followed Spock into the lift.

'Bexley,' she said, more firmly this time.

The lift seemed to accept my dog's word as a command. It began moving.

When the doors opened, Spock set off confidently.

'Do you actually know where you're going or are you just making it up as you go along?'

'Bexley,' she replied without turning to look at me.

A minute or two later, I ducked through the door into the engine room – well, to what I assumed was the engine room. It was marginally less shiny clean and glossy white than what I'd seen of the rest of the ship. A pulsating column of light rising from a white base occupied most of the centre of the room. But no Bexley.

Spock headed straight to a door in the corner. A small purple light next to the door indicated the toilet was occupied.

A moment later, Bexley emerged from the room, looking uncharacteristically embarrassed. That was odd; she hadn't shown any indication of being ashamed of bodily functions in the past. Or was I judging her by unfair standards?

'Oh, hey, you two.' She held one hand-hoof behind herself and brushed her forelock over her face with the other. 'I … um … I wasn't expecting you to join me here.' She hastened to the central column, then elbow-checked something to make a drawer eject. Bending low over the drawer, she held both hand-hooves up to her long muzzle. 'I'm just checking the crystals to see if they have enough va-va-voom to get us to Magrathea.' She blew on whatever was in the drawer. 'And … see! There we have it. There was life left in them after all.'

She straightened herself and motioned for me to look in the drawer, backing away so it would be safe for me to approach. It looked a bit like the drawer in a washing machine. And it was filled with what looked for all the world like detergent – coarse white powder with a few dots of translucent brightly coloured crystals.

Spock stood up on her hind legs to take a sniff but dropped back down onto all fours dejectedly a moment later. 'Not food.'

I arched an eyebrow as I looked across the room at Bexley.

She was sort of tap-dancing – her feet making a clippity-clop on the smooth surface of the floor. 'What can you smell? And do you see the glowing bits? Oh, um, I don't know how sensitive your biology is. I mean, your nose is so ridiculously small – maybe you can't detect odours.'

'Smells like laundry detergent – which is funny because that's exactly what it looks like.'

She pushed her forelock over her face with a hand-hoof. 'Huh. Okay, that's weird. It doesn't smell like impatience to you?'

'Yes,' said Spock, catching me off guard.

I shook my head, then remembered Bexley didn't know what that meant. 'No, er… Impatience doesn't have a smell.'

She burst out laughing. 'Ha. Good one.' Her nostrils flared and she sucked in air. 'Oh! You really think that. Oh, wow. Okay. And you don't see it? That's weird because you seem to have pretty good visual acuity, so maybe it's more of a different light-spectrum thing. Actually, that's interesting because I have a theory that the mechanism of—'

The door to the engine room slid open again. BB lifted her wings in greeting. 'Hello, you three. My AI said I'd find you here. I'm ready to get back to work in the lab. Good news, Lem. I think I'll have your drug ready later today.'

Bexley pushed the drawer shut. 'Oh, that's amazing. I'm so excited for you, Lem! Even if you don't take me up on a hump or a hug, it's still going to make your life so much easier.' Without pausing to let me respond, she added, 'Hey, AI. Put me through to Henry, please.'

There was a brief pause before Henry's smooth, posh accent and her characteristically hostile voice sounded from my watch. 'What's up, bags of foetid water? Calling to admit defeat?'

Bexley spluttered and stamped her foot. 'Um, no, thank you, actually. I'm calling to say it worked. Some of the crystals still had a charge. It won't get us to the other side of the galaxy, but it's plenty to get us to Magrathea.'

'Those crystals were bone plugging dry,' said Henry. 'How the pluck did you manage that?'

'Well, obviously they weren't, you ... you silly robot, you. It's not like I can just ... you know, magic up some sort of crystal-reinvigorating substance. I can't violate the laws of physics, duh.' Bexley kicked the floor and pushed her mane down over her forehead. 'So, you can just go ahead and take us to warp now, pilot. We should ... um ... be able to sustain warp three for almost six hours.'

'I thought you said the, er ... the Firefly class could maintain warp four?' I took a step towards Bexley – which was obviously a mistake, as I felt a familiar tickle in my throat.

Bexley tapped her hand-hoof in mid-air. 'We can, yes. Good memory. But I didn't ... um ... find enough charged crystals. If we went at warp four, we'd fall back out of warp when we were still, like, twelve weeks away from Magrathea. If we keep it to warp three, we'll get there in about four hours instead of one – but at least we'll get there today.'

And then I started sneezing and couldn't stop.

BB took a step forwards. 'All right, Lem, let's get you back to medlab and focus on getting you healthy.'

With each successive sneeze, my spasms got bigger. 'Good luck,' called Bexley as we headed out.

BB raised her wings, revealing the little arms at waist height that were normally concealed beneath them. The talons reached out and supported me gently as she ushered me out of the engine room.

———

Less than an hour later, I was once again recovering in my comically too-short bed in the medlab and worrying about the state of my pyjamas. It was bad enough hanging around this prison ship in my filthy jim-jams. I couldn't make my very first visit to an alien world smelling like I'd spent the last three months living under Spock's bed. *Am I even going to be going to Magrathea? Are we all going? Should some of us wait on the Teapot? How will we decide?*

'Hey, Doc,' I began. 'I don't suppose there's anywhere around here I could get some clean clothes, is there? I've been wearing my pyjamas for the best part of three days now and they're getting a bit rank.'

BB clucked her beak. 'Ah, yes, of course. One moment.' She waddled to a cupboard in the far corner of the room and retrieved a bundle of cloth. Returning to my bed, she unfolded the neat stack – and revealed it to be a large square of fabric. She spread it over me. 'There you go.'

Aurora drifted into the room through the open door. 'Hello, my dears. We've still got about three hours to go before we get to Magrathea, so I thought I'd check if anyone had specific requests for lunch.'

Spock's tail wagged frantically and she ran a sort of infinity symbol through Aurora. 'Vindaloo, please, friend.'

Aurora glowed a mix of royal blue and green – with little flecks of purple where Spock touched her.

'Hey, Aurora. Er…' I didn't think I could take another bowl of garlic, but I couldn't think of what I did want. 'Could I please get … er…' Everyone looked at me, but I couldn't think what I wanted so I just snatched at the first idea that wandered through the void of my mind. 'Can I have a Welsh rarebit, please?'

Aurora faded almost to invisibility. 'I'm sorry, Lem. I must have misheard. You want to eat a bunnyboo? I know they held you captive against your will, but that seems a bit of an overreaction, no?'

It took me a second to figure out that the translator must have gone wrong. 'No, not a rabbit, a rarebit.' BB looked at me blankly, Spock tilted her head to the side, and Aurora shifted into a magenta hue. 'I know it sounds like I'm saying the same word, but they're not. They're er ... homophones. Two different words that sound the same, but have different meanings like Greece and grease or er ... four candles and fork handles.'

Bexley appeared at the doorway, twirling her mane around her hand-hoof. 'There are four lights?'

BB shuffled around, making her preparations. 'Your language uses the same word to mean more than one thing? Is there a shortage of sounds that your species can make?'

I nodded at Bexley's question and shrugged at BB's – then remembered they wouldn't understand either of those responses. 'Sorry, yes, we reuse words. Sometimes they're spelt the same and sometimes not, but yes. Anyway, I don't know why we do it. It's not logical – but who ever said the human race was logical?'

Fuchsia was still her dominant colour, but the rest of Aurora's rainbow began to emerge. 'Ah, I see. Well, I shall endeavour to create a reneging bunnyboo for you, whatever it might be.'

'Thank you, Aurora. I'm sure it will be lovely.' I had no idea what I was going to get for lunch. Hurrying to change the subject, I said, 'Er ... BB, just before Aurora got here, I asked you if there were any clean clothes.'

BB clucked her beak and gestured with a wing at me. 'Yes, and I brought you some. You're welcome.'

'Thank you, yes. Except something's getting lost in translation. These aren't clothes – they're blankets.'

BB turned to face Aurora and then Spock.

'Blanket,' said Spock, jumping up to sit next to me on the bed.

'I'm sorry, my dear,' said Aurora. 'I'm not sure my friend or I understand your meaning. You requested clean bedding and the doctor provided some. What are we missing?'

'Not bedding.' I was starting to feel like this conversation was getting away from me. 'Clothes.' I waved my hands over myself. 'For my body.'

BB and Aurora looked at one another, apparently confused by what I thought was a simple request.

'Towels, you guys! She wants towels.' Bexley stood at the door but refrained from stepping into the room.

BB clucked her beak. 'Oh, I'm so sorry. There must be a glitch in the translation matrix. Yes, of course, towels are in the cupboard in the bathroom.'

Even as they spoke, it hit me. No one else on the ship wore clothes. Spock had a collar. The others had jewellery – which, now that I thought about it, probably housed their translators. But no one wore clothes.

'No, sorry, not a towel,' I said, struggling to think how I was going to explain this. 'My people wear clothes – like armour, but soft. It protects us and keeps us warm. Also, we don't generally walk around naked, even if the temperature would allow it. We just don't – it's considered immodest.'

They all gawped at me like I'd grown Zaphod Beeblebrox's second head. 'It's partially about warmth, but also our skin is quite sensitive. I mean, mine is more sensitive than the average person's – but even still. Most always people wear clothes, even when we're at home alone.'

'You wear armour all the time?' Bexley looked horrified.

BB fluffed up her feathers. 'And it covers your entire body?'

'Well, yeah. But not like hard, uncomfortable armour. It's soft and without it, we feel ... that is, at least, I feel ... er ... naked.'

'Naked?' All three of them spoke in unison. Spock picked that moment to underline the word by licking herself.

'Well, exposed, I guess. We do hide behind our clothes.' I drummed my fingers on my lip as I tried to figure out a way to convey why humans wore clothes. 'We do. Clothes are partially about hiding our private parts, hiding our true selves, covering ourselves up. But it's a protective thing, too. Protection from cold, from discomfort, from irritants, from germs.'

Bexley brushed her forelock over her long face. 'That seems like a really weird evolutionary development. What would be the advantage for a species that needs armour it can't produce for itself?'

Biting down on my lip, I struggled to keep from laughing – or maybe crying. 'I don't actually know. You're absolutely right, of course. It doesn't make sense that we need clothes, but we do.' There was no way I was going to delve into the depths of my dysphoria with all these virtual strangers. Weirdly, unlike most people I'd known on Earth, I didn't think my new friends would judge me – or worse yet, pity me. Hell, I didn't even know how sex and gender worked in their respective societies.

Leaning forwards, I allowed my head to fall into my hands. I couldn't walk around naked. No way. I couldn't bring myself to do it – but also, even if I had no psychological issue with it, between my allergies and the fact I was always cold... No. Not an option.

I ran a hand through my hair. 'I'm sorry.' I pinched my

lips together, determined not to let myself cry. I just wanted to go home.

Bexley took a step towards me again, then stopped herself.

Aurora shimmered all the colours of the rainbow and coasted over to me. 'No, you mustn't apologise for being yourself. You require fitted blanket-armour to wear and, by stars, you shall have it.' One of her edges passed over my face, which tickled.

BB fluffed her facial feathers. 'Whether your reasons are physiological, psychological, or merely a case of what you're used to … we want you to be comfortable.'

'These blankets,' Aurora said, waving at the extra blankets BB had laid over me, 'is the fabric suitable to you?'

I ran my fingers over the soft cotton-like material. 'Yeah. I'll figure out a way to tie them to myself.' I snorted back my tears and wiped my eyes with the back of my hands.

'No, no, my dear.' As Aurora spoke, BB picked the cloth up. 'If you'll be so kind as to authorise your AI to transmit details of your preferred fit, measurements, and cut, I should be able to make something suitable for you before we arrive at Magrathea.'

I wiped my face with with the back of my hand again. Here I was, getting ready to visit an alien world, surrounded by people who'd been nothing but kind and accommodating – and all I could do was blub about the state of my clothes. *For pity's sake – how pathetic am I?*

I just wanted to go home.

BB danced side to side, bobbing her head. 'Now ordinarily, you understand, this drug would go through extensive testing before being tried on a person. And even then, I'd want to try it on a set of healthy volunteers long before I tried it on someone who might actually need it. Obviously, I've run quite a few virtual trials and I'm going to start you on a low dose – but I'm not an expert in your species. I'm guided largely by the information gleaned from your own brain.'

'Whoa whoa whoa. Wait just one bastarding second. Could this hurt me? How did the virtual trials go? What's in this stuff? I have questions!'

From the door, Bexley nickered. 'Way to sell it, Doc. She's really going to want to try it after that pitch.'

Spock stuck her head into my armpit and whined.

BB turned to Bexley and clucked her beak. 'There's no need for sarcasm. Consent is worthless if it's not informed.' She looked at me. 'I'm not trying to dissuade you of anything, Lem. Rather, I'm simply doing my duty to ensure you have all the facts. I believe this drug is safe. In fact, it is my view that it is in your best interests to consent to treatment –

however, it is entirely your decision to make. Please do not interpret my remarks as an attempt to pressure you in one direction or the other.'

Bexley did a little dance. 'But if you have it and it works, then I can stop worrying that I'm going to accidentally kill you! Because I can't tell you how many times I've almost run across the room to hug you and then I have to stop myself before I do so I don't end up hurting you. But, I swear, I just think you're a really amazing person. And Spock says you give great snuggles.'

I'd never had anyone make such a big and obvious deal about wanting to be my friend. It was endearing – maybe a bit overwhelming. *Deep breath.* 'Load me up, Doc,' I said. 'Let's give it a go.'

With no further fanfare, BB pushed the solution in through the IV port in my arm. 'Let that work for a few minutes and then we'll test it out.'

Bexley practically squealed. 'I can finally hug Lem.'

BB pivoted awkwardly on one claw and extended the other in a sort of stop gesture. 'Whoa there, Captain Zealous! There will be no hugging – not yet anyway. When I said we would test, I meant we'd expose Lem to one of your hairs under controlled conditions. If that goes well, then I'll allow you to move within a metre.'

Bexley stamped her hooves on the floor. 'But I want a hug!'

Spock jumped off the bed and ran to her, wagging her tail excitedly. 'Spock hug Bexley friend!'

BB fluttered her wings. 'There you go, Mx Impatient. You've got your hug. Now I'll thank you to stay at least three metres away from my patient.' She dilated her eyes. 'Until we can be certain this treatment works, obviously. Then you can do whatever you mutually consent to for the duration of the treatment's effectiveness – which should be about a day.'

Tapping the door frame with her hand-hooves, Bexley said, 'Right, well, I'm going to go see about some lunch.'

Spock wagged her tail excitedly. 'Feed Spock?'

'We should be along shortly,' I said. 'Spock, you can go with Bexley if you like. I'm sure Aurora will be happy to feed you.' I didn't need to tell her twice. She grabbed her brain from the bed and trotted off after Bexley.

BB tapped the IV line. 'Indeed.'

———

When we arrived in the lounge less than an hour later, Bexley was eating and chatting with Aurora. Spock was curled up on the floor by Bexley's feet, licking her brain.

Aurora glowed turquoise and green. 'Hello, friends. Lem, I wasn't sure which you'd want first, so I've got both ready on that tray there.'

I followed her nub to a covered dish, a mug, and a large, uneven stack of cloth.

Bexley leapt up off the sofa, still chewing her lunch as she proclaimed, 'I made the, um, hoof protectors.'

I lifted the cloth to discover what was underneath – the reason the bundle looked so large and lumpy. 'Shoes? You made me shoes?'

Bexley blew air out her nostrils. 'Okay, I don't know what word you're saying right now. The best my translator can come up with is a word that means a little insert we sometimes put in the centre of our hooves to protect the delicate flesh there if we're going to be walking a long way on sharp gravel.'

I held up the shoes: they looked like those foam shoes I'd

always hated – but they were rainbow coloured and they looked like my size. I slid them on over my filthy socks. 'Oh my days, Bexley! These are amazing. They're the most comfortable shoes I've ever worn.'

Bexley knocked the sides of her hand-hooves together in a kind of clapping motion. 'Sweet! I wasn't really sure how they worked, but it seemed like they were kind of part protection and part cushioning. Using the preference data in your file plus the scans of your hooves plus your mass … well, and then I kind of extrapolated. I'm so glad you like them. They're not too ugly, are they?'

Honestly, they were, but I didn't care. 'They're perfect.' The bundle of cloth contained a clean new set of … pyjamas. I stepped into the loo to put them on. They were soft, warm, comfortable, and clean. And they fit perfectly. What more could a person ask for?

When I returned in my new togs, Bexley was dancing from foot to foot. 'Hey, you.'

I was overcome by a sense of shyness. 'Bexley.'

She lifted her arms. 'Come here.' She ran across the room and enveloped me in her strong arms. I was overcome with joy and relief. I hadn't had a hug like that in … far too long. She embraced me like a blanket. My shyness melted away. She held me, patting my back and stroking my hair until Aurora brought in lunch for BB and me.

Another cup of tea and a bowl of Welsh rarebit-flavoured soupy porridge. Weird. *Must remember to request foods with the right texture.* The mushy mix of bread, cheese, and mustard messed with my head.

I forced myself to swallow a lumpy mouthful. 'So, how long until we get to Magrathea?'

Bexley lifted the pendant hanging around her neck, confirming my guess it housed her AI. 'Um, about an hour and a half.' I sat down on the sofa next to her. She reached out a hand-hoof towards me. 'May I?'

Instinctively, I raised a hand to my head protectively. 'You want to touch my hair?'

She tapped her hoof on her knee. 'Please?'

I chuckled. 'Er, sure, I guess.' She was surprisingly gentle. 'So, what's the plan? When we get there, I mean. How do we get down to the planet?' My shoulders fell as a thought occurred to me. 'Actually, who's going?'

The thought of visiting a new planet both terrified and thrilled me. Though, weirdly, the balance had shifted more towards exhilaration now that I had clean, new clothes. The idea of staying on the ship while everyone else went to the planet didn't make me feel safe; it produced a strange longing in me.

'Well,' she said, still playing with my hair. 'That'll depend on what we find when we arrive, I guess. We'll scan their signals to see what we can find out about them. What we learn can guide us in terms of where we can go and who should be on the mission.'

'Do we land the ship?'

Aurora floated near the door. 'Ah, no. That's not advisable. Landing may not kill us – but we'd certainly not be in any fit state to take off again.'

Bexley leant back away from me. 'One does not simply fly a Firefly class ship into an atmosphere. The *Teapot* is very much not designed for the abuses of atmospheric pressure.'

BB took several steps towards Aurora. 'As for how we get there…' The bare skin on her cheeks flushed – though I had no idea what that meant in her species. 'Aurora tells me this ship is equipped with four transporters.'

My eyes went wide. 'We can beam down to the surface?'

Bexley stopped playing with my hair. 'I have no idea what you just said.'

'Beam – like, matter to energy conversion and back again,' I said – feeling very foolish.

'Oh gosh! That's amazing. Can your people really do that? That would be phenomenal – just think what we could achieve if—'

I held my hands up in surrender. 'Sorry, no. My bad. I jumped to conclusions when BB said we could transport down. So, what does it mean to *transport* then? How does it work?'

Bexley and BB both opened their mouths as if to speak and then closed them. 'Um,' said Bexley after a moment. 'It's probably best if you ask your AI.'

I'd forgotten that was an option. 'Help me out here, Holly?'

'Of course, Lem. How may I be of assistance?'

Huh. 'What's a transporter, please?'

'A transporter is sort of like a virtual pneumatic tube crossed with a tractor beam.'

I scrunched up my face. 'A what with a what?'

'A virtual pneumatic tube crossed with a tractor beam,' Holly repeated.

'No, but how does it work?'

'Please clarify: are you seeking a technical explanation or a user's perspective?'

I forced air out through my mouth. 'Save the techie bit for another time. Just the basics, please.'

'A transporter pod is a small engineless craft – usually designed for a single occupant. It is propelled between two points using magic.'

'Magic!' I leapt out of my seat. 'We have magic?'

'Don't be ridiculous,' replied Holly, 'of course not. But

any sufficiently advanced technology is indistinguishable from magic. It is one of your human thinkers who said that. Is it not true?'

I shook my head. 'Clarke's third law. Yeah, yeah. I get you.' I looked at Bexley again. 'So, transporters, eh?'

The lift doors slid open, delivering us to the bridge.

'Hey, Henry,' called Bexley as she trotted across the open space towards the robot. Spock followed her out and ran straight to Henry, giving her a thorough sniffing.

'Cheese curds,' replied Henry by way of greeting in that way-too-posh androgynous voice of hers. 'While you've been downstairs playing house, I've been doing the offing research. And bringing us into orbit around the planet. Where are the gas bag and the feather duster?'

'Aurora and BB will join us in a bit,' I said as I stood gawping at the incredible view of the dome above us. 'They're just cleaning up the lunch stuff.'

'You meatsacks waste so much time with your biological processes. Do you have any idea how forking inefficient you are? Do you even care?'

'Whatever, you snarctastic household appliance,' said Bexley without even looking in her direction. 'You're just jealous. But since you're obviously dying to tell us what you've learnt, go ahead and enlighten us.'

Henry extended something that looked like a whisk in Bexley's direction and – well – whisked it a bit. 'The planet has both gravity and air that are similar to what we have on the ship – within the tolerances of the requirements of all the generic pork products on board.'

'Within the tolerances,' I repeated – intending it as a sort of question.

'Oh good, it's mastered the art of repetition.'

Bexley and Spock both moved rapidly to put themselves between Henry and me.

'Be nice,' said Spock.

Bexley pointed a hand-hoof at Henry. 'Lem is a person – same as you. She has feelings and she's worthy of respect – just like anyone else. Let her be. She's as sentient as you or me or Spock.'

'Well, that's debatable. Anyway, did you want to hear more about the planet you're about to visit – or would you rather stand around for a bit longer debating the intellectual capacity of this ham sandwich?'

'Just tell us about the planet,' I snapped. Spock wandered over to the window and gazed out at the planet below us. This time it really did fill almost half the view.

An appendage that looked like a bottle opener popped out of Henry's torso. 'Sure, fine, whatever. It seems we're in a bit of a void between various systems. Magrathea has been visited by any number of spacefaring races. The locals have profited from their position as a sort of roadside services for interstellar travellers. At any given time, dozens of different species can be found in the planet's restaurants, engine repair facilities, and whorehouses.'

Bexley tapped the nearest console excitedly. 'Sweet, so we're not going to freak them out with the general freakery of our appearance? I was a bit worried. You know, 'cause I don't know if you've noticed but we're a bit of a mixed bag of, um, pick 'n' mix. Like, have you even seen us?'

'A horse, an unswearing robot, a giant parrot, a cloud of sentient glitter gas, a non-binary IT project manager, and a talking dog walk into a bar…' A startled snigger escaped my lips – I hadn't meant to say any of that. But once I'd opened my mouth, I couldn't stop the words – or the hysterical laughter that followed. I slapped a hand over my mouth.

'AI, call BB. Lem's having another attack. The drug isn't working,' Bexley bellowed. Unable to speak coherently, I flailed my arms wildly to get her attention. Unfortunately, that seemed to worry her more. 'Hurry!'

Biting down on my lip, I took a deep breath and held it as long as I could. 'I'm sorry. I'm sorry. I'm okay.' With the sleeve of my new blanket top, I wiped the tears streaming from my eyes. 'It's just … an attack of the giggles.'

Bexley's massive jaw fell slack. 'That … ridiculous sound … that was you laughing? I thought you were dying!' She punched me in the shoulder. Hard.

I was still biting my cheek to keep more giggles from escaping. 'Sorry,' I said through clenched teeth.

She full-on brayed in response. Both of us collapsed to the floor, laughing uncontrollably. When the lift doors opened a few moments later, BB burst out with Aurora drifting urgently behind.

BB ran straight to me, medkit in hand. 'I was so sure that drug would work.' She paused. 'Bexley? You're affected too? Oh dear. Spock, Henry, have these two been poisoned?'

Spock ran over. 'Lem silly.' She licked me.

Henry turned herself in circles at the pilot's station. 'What my furry friend is trying to say is that the attack this pair is suffering from is a psychological one, not a physiological one.'

Both Bexley and I squealed with more laughter at that. BB cooed and clucked and attempted to scan us with some sort of device. 'Elevated heart rates, elevated respiration, but oxygenation appears normal for your respective species. What is going on here?' Her wings popped out as she jabbed the little talon-hands under them into her sides.

Finally regaining some of my self-control, I managed to reply, 'I'm so sorry, Doc. We were discussing plans for going down to the planet and I was overcome by the strangeness of the whole situation. I started laughing and then I couldn't stop.'

Aurora glowed a mix of yellow and blue. 'This is laughter? You gave my ... friend the fright of her life because you found the precarious nature of our escape from the bunnyboos ... funny?' The yellow began to recede, leaving blue as her dominant colour.

I composed my features as best I could. 'I'm sorry.' Spock licked my face.

Bexley stood on all fours, looking even more like a tiny horse. She hung her head low and wagged her tail slowly. 'I really am sorry, BB. I freaked out because I didn't understand what was happening to Lem – but then when I worked it out, I got caught up in it. I really didn't mean to alarm you. It's just when you think about it, we *are* kind of ridiculous.' I reached down to put my hand on Bexley's shoulder. 'Don't,' she said. 'You'll set me off again.'

Aurora was a shockingly vivid shade of blue.

BB made a little jerky motion with her head, fluffing her feathers. 'Well, I suppose I am relieved to know the drug is holding as well as I'd hoped.' Her pupils dilated and contracted repeatedly. 'Well, go on then – what have you learnt about this planet?'

Aurora hovered next to BB. 'If you feel confident you can relay it without being overcome by the hilarity of our plight, that is.'

'Maybe I should field this one while the frogspawn recover from their little episode of asphaltery,' said Henry.

I focused on my breathing while Henry told them what she'd learnt. At one point, I glanced over at Bexley, but I very nearly succumbed to the giggles again, so I resolved not to look at her until I was sure I was over it.

'So,' Bexley began. I had to remind myself not to turn towards her. 'How do we decide who goes down to the planet and who stays on the ship? Firefly classes are equipped with four transporters, so four of us can go and two will remain with the ship.'

Henry extended a screwdriver, which whirred as she spoke. 'Spock is the one who most closely resembles the planet's native species, so I suggest she goes with the landing party.'

Bexley tapped a hand-hoof on the floor. 'Agreed. And I need to find something I can use to recharge the crystals.'

'Well, Spock's not going anywhere without me,' I said.

BB put her hands on her hips. 'If my patient is going, then I'd better go too – just to be on the safe side. You should be fine, but I'd hate for you to have a reaction to something you encounter on the ground.'

I nodded. 'Thanks.'

'I'm not able to leave the ship anyway,' said Aurora.

'Well, that's four then,' said Henry in a dry, overly sarcastic tone. 'Lucky you. What a funny coincidence – it's the meatsacks. Who could have predicted that?'

'Did you want to go, Henry? Maybe we can reconsider,' I said.

A little plunger emerged from Henry and vibrated. 'Actually, it's probably best if I stay on the ship. If we need to get away quickly, we'll need a pilot at the helm.'

Bexley flared her nostrils and breathed noisily. 'Pffff! We won't need to leave in a rush. It's a straightforward shopping trip with a side of information gathering. What could go wrong?'

The transporter bay was on the ship's lowest level, around the corner from the engine room. It was a smallish space, lined with what looked like blue phone boxes. I couldn't help but chuckle. 'Are they bigger on the inside?'

'No,' Bexley replied in all seriousness. 'Of course not. Are you sure you're feeling okay?'

I waved the idea away. 'Never mind. Earth thing.'

Bexley glanced at me askance. 'Your people sure seem to want to violate the laws of physics a lot.'

Henry shoved her way into the room and wheeled past me. 'Right, listen up, meatheads. For those of you who've not used a plucking transporter, the rules are pretty simple. Even a high street bank's chatbot could follow them. Even an idiot.' She stabbed a nail file in my direction. 'Get comfy, strap in, let me do the driving. Any questions?'

I looked around to see if anyone else was going to speak. 'Er, yes. What do we do in case of emergency?'

'If there's an emergency,' Henry began.

'Yes?'

'Then you die, sandwich,' Henry said. 'How about that? That do it for you?'

I stopped mid-step towards one of the pods. 'And that's supposed to make me feel safe? You want me to strap myself – and my dog – into these things without any kind of assurance that it's not a death trap?'

BB put one of her shoulder-hands on my elbow. 'Transporter technology may be new to you, but it's been safely used for centuries by many species.'

Bexley encircled me in her arms. 'I checked the maintenance logs. They've been regularly serviced.' Being held by her made me feel unexpectedly safe.

'Henry and I will check you're all strapped in safely,' said Aurora. 'And then Henry will deliver you to a pod-parking station near Magrathea's largest market town. From there, it should be about a quarter-of-an-hour walk to the market.'

Henry revved her wheels impatiently. 'Now remember, you're there to get unobtainium to recharge the crystals, parts to repair the ansible, star maps, and any information you can glean about this sector or the bunnyboos. No shopping for' – she extended a hose towards me – 'pretty blankets.'

BB flicked the tip of a wing at Henry in a dismissive gesture. 'Based on the data feed we've had from the planet, they're in need of certain medicines and lack the technology to create them.' Her cheeks flushed pinkish again. 'Aurora helped me prepare a selection of the most-needed ones. We have those to trade – amongst other things.'

Aurora drifted to the centre of the room, one edge of her fluttering through BB's wings. 'Now, into your pods and get going.'

Bexley kissed me gently on the cheek – tickling my face with her whiskers. 'It's going to be okay, Lem, I promise.'

She patted Spock on the head and then picked a pod and climbed in.

I opened a pod door and peered in. It was filled with that strange gel that was in the stasis pods – it looked and felt like it ought to be liquid, but it acted more like memory foam. When I pressed it, it moulded itself to my hand. 'Well, in you get, Spock.'

Spock looked at me with apprehension. 'Don't wanna.' She trembled.

'It'll be okay, mate.' I laid a reassuring hand on her head. 'We'll be together again as soon as we land.' It was like the flight to Canada all over again. I'd felt so guilty as I shoved her into the crate. Hopefully, this would be shorter. Plus, this time I could explain. 'We're going for a ride. It'll only be a few minutes.'

'Car ride?' Her tail wagged tentatively.

'Kind of like a car ride. But we go in separate vehicles.'

Her ears folded back. 'Not ride together?' She shoved her face between my knees.

'It's okay, I promise.' I really, really hoped I wasn't lying. 'Just get in. I'll see you again when we're on the planet. Better leave the brain behind though. Aurora will take good care of it for you.' I didn't want Spock dropping it some-where we couldn't retrieve it from.

Spock unclamped her jaw from the toy reluctantly. She tucked her tail between her legs and climbed into the pod. Once BB had shown me how to secure Spock's seatbelt, we each chose one of the remaining pods. Henry checked I'd secured myself properly, then closed the door. It was a good thing I wasn't claustrophobic. The pod was only big enough to hold me. The gel made it comfy, but there was no getting around the tight squeeze.

I'm actually sitting in an alien pod that's about to take me to a planet. A planet that's not Earth. Although I was equal parts excited and terrified, I tried my best to stay focused. This little excursion could help me find my way home.

I was surprised at how clear Henry's voice was – but of course it was: my watch was in the pod with me. 'Ready?'

'As I'll ever be.' I started counting primes.

Imagine combining a roller coaster with a sensory deprivation chamber. That's what it's like being transported – fine for packages; not so fine for corporeals.

After a period of time that felt like hours – but also mere milliseconds – but which, according to my watch, was actually eighteen minutes, I came to a halt. No feelings of deceleration or crashing or anything like that. Just, suddenly, I realised I wasn't moving anymore.

'Any of you cream puffs dead?' queried a disembodied voice.

'I am, Henry,' I replied.

'Oh dear? Hang on, I'm coming for you, Lem.'

'It's okay, Doc. I was being *figurative.* I think I'm all right. If you get out before me, could you check on Spock, please?'

'Figurative? You mean hyperbolic? Yes, of course. Hang on,' BB said. 'I'm out. I'll check on Spock.' There was a pause while, presumably, she did as she said.

'Hello, friend,' came Spock's frantic voice. 'Where Lem?'

'We can go get her, right now,' replied BB.

'I'm here, Spock. It's okay.'

'Where? No see.' I should have known better than to reply when she couldn't tell where my voice was coming from.

There was a click and the door swung open. For some reason, I was shocked to discover I was upright. I spotted Spock running around frantically, looking for me.

'Spock,' I called. She ran to my pod and leapt into my

arms, covering me with kisses. 'All right, all right. Let me get up.'

'Spock worry.' She jumped down to the ground outside the pod.

I climbed out and joined her, setting foot onto my very first alien world. It looked like a perfectly ordinary small town car park – except the sky was green. The air smelt a bit weird – sort of peppery. I only wobbled slightly. 'Thanks, Doc. Hey, where's Bexley?'

BB lifted her wings in greeting. 'Her pod is just behind yours.'

I steadied myself and the three of us walked over to the fourth pod. BB opened the door to reveal Bexley – sound asleep with her eyes wide open.

'It's best to let her come round naturally,' said the doctor.

'How long is that like—' I began, but I was cut off by Bexley snorting loudly and leaping out of her pod.

'Hey, hey, hi.' She shook her head repeatedly like she was trying to jog something loose. 'Sorry, areion don't react well to travelling by transporter. Rapid changes in altitude mess with our equilibrium. I probably should have mentioned that beforehand, eh? How long was I out?'

She pranced about on all fours for a minute or so. Eventually, she stood upright, shook her head, and walked over to us, neighing and sweeping her long, silky mane back over her shoulders. 'Wow. Right. I swear I could eat an entire hay-bale right now.' Spock's ears perked up at the mention of food. 'I'm so wired. Okay, what's first? Where do we start?'

Just then a … an … the only word that came to mind was *dog*. A massive russet-coloured Brussels griffon. Floppy ears, stubby face, and long beard. The creature walked over and called out to us. Standing on all fours, she – I stuck with *she* because I still hadn't figured out how to distinguish alien genders — was taller than the others. Almost as tall as I was. Very nearly the size of a horse — or at least a pony. I wouldn't want to get into a fight with her.

'Greetings, stranger.' She bowed to Spock and ignored the rest of us. 'Welcome to the Land and Dash pod park. We have different rates for hourly, daily, and monthly parkers.'

As she spoke, I glimpsed the rounded teeth of a herbivore. *Hopefully that means I won't have to fight any of them.*

I shushed my brain.

BB stepped forwards and lifted her wings. 'Greetings to you, new friend.' The creature looked startled to be addressed by a giant parrot but seemed to roll with it. 'We will be staying just a few hours. And could you point us in the direction of somewhere that would allow us to trade some of our goods for local currency?'

The furry creature addressed her words once more to Spock. 'With our multi-pod discount, it will be six quid per seventy-two-minute period or part thereof. If you're likely to be more than twelve seventy-two-minute periods, then it will be worthwhile to pay for a full day.'

Bexley whinnied and stepped towards the parking attendant. 'Thank you. We shouldn't be longer than four periods, so the hourly rate is fine. We'd be grateful if you could direct us to somewhere we can convert our goods for trade into currency. Also, if you know a place to purchase engine and ansible parts, maps – we'd be grateful.'

Steadfastly refusing to address anyone but Spock, the attendant replied. 'If you head in that direction' – she gestured with her stubby snoot – 'you'll come to a pawnshop on your right. Third street along. Blue sign out front. Shouldn't take you more than eighteen minutes or so. I don't fix engines or ansibles, or go anywhere.' She turned and headed back to the booth at the centre of the lot.

We all thanked the attendant and began the walk into town. Aside from the green sky, the only other main difference to an Earth town was the size of the buildings. They were mostly one storey, with squat low doors and windows, but much bigger than you'd find on Earth – even in Canada.

I tried not to stare as we passed more of the same species. Some were a bit bigger; some smaller. They ranged in colour from a mousy grey to a darker red-brown. Most of them ignored us completely. The odd one muttered cursory greetings to Spock. Never to me or the other two – only Spock. The roads were paved with a charcoal-coloured substance. The pavements were wider than you'd typically see on Earth – presumably to accommodate the locals' bulk.

About a quarter of an hour later – just when I was beginning to suspect the parking attendant had led us astray, we found the pawnshop. I pushed open the door and we all walked in. A biped with pale turquoise skin and tufts of bright pink fur covering much of her body was leaving the shop just as we arrived. Her eyes went wide as she passed us, but she didn't say anything.

A couple of bored-looking quadrupeds stood behind a counter.

BB walked towards them, clutching her bag to her side. 'Greetings, new friends. How are you this fine afternoon?'

Without looking up, one of them – I couldn't tell which – said, 'Hello.'

'Okay, yes, well my companions and I have just arrived on your fascinating planet. We're in need of some local currency. We brought goods to trade. Are you in a position to assist us?'

One of the creatures looked up, took all of us in, then sat there, blinking and not saying anything.

I noticed BB and Bexley both turn their attention to their

own translators just as Holly's voice reached my ears – lower in volume than usual, but still recognisably the voice Holly reserved for itself. 'Lem, I have made an observation about the indigenous population's use of language. Is now a convenient time to relay it?'

I glanced at the creatures again, but they'd gone back to … the nothing it was they'd been doing when we came in. 'Er, sure. What is it?'

'Their language doesn't seem to allow for the concept of questions. Compared to most sentient species I am aware of, they lack the capacity for curiosity. They neither ask questions nor understand the purpose of them. Anything phrased as a question is likely to be disregarded.'

'Ah.' I scratched my head. 'Folks, I think we might need to try a different tack.'

Bexley and BB both moved closer. The four of us – including Spock – gathered in a tight-knit ring in the centre of the shop. 'Yeah,' said Bexley. 'We got the no-questions news too. Right, lemme try.'

She walked to the counter and placed her hand-hooves on its surface. 'Hi there. We're new here and we need to obtain currency in order to buy supplies for our ship. We've brought stuff to trade for currency. Are you, um… That is, please have a look at what we've brought.'

The two beings – I decided to call them pakleds – looked at one another and then past Bexley at Spock. 'We will look at your goods.'

'Hello, friends,' said Spock.

'Hello,' they replied in unison.

'Hello,' repeated Spock.

I had a feeling this would go on all day if I let it, so I took a step towards BB and motioned for her to unpack the contents of her bag.

She took the satchel from her shoulder and set it on the counter and began removing contents. She set a number of jars, bottles, and pots on the surface. Neither of the pakleds moved. After a moment, BB picked a bottle up. 'This is, um, oh, yes, this is maple syrup.' She touched another bottle. 'And this one is cayenne pepper. Both add a lovely flavour to food – though in different ways.'

'Flavour serves no purpose,' said one of the pakleds.

BB clucked her beak. 'I see. Okay, I'll put the seasonings away then if they're not useful to you.' She packed some of the bottles away. 'This one is a medicine that can be used to treat Bowden's malady and this one treats space mumps.'

'These are drugs,' said one of the pakleds. Obviously, it wasn't a question.

BB fluffed her feathers. 'That is correct.'

'Show us your licence to manufacture and sell drugs on Magrathea.'

BB rocked her head back. 'I assure you I am a highly qualified physician. I was trained on Brontitall and have worked on no less than six different planets, treating dozens of species.'

'Show us your licence to manufacture and sell drugs on Magrathea,' the pakled repeated.

I sighed impatiently. How were we going to get the supplies we needed to get home if we couldn't get any local currency?

11 / THE MERCHANDISE

Twenty minutes later, we walked back out the pawnshop's door, money in hand. Well, not literally in hand, obviously. It was tucked away in Bexley and BB's respective bags.

'I cannot believe I had to sell my body to those cretins,' BB half-squawked.

Bexley groaned. 'Again. You did *not* sell your body. Stop saying that.'

BB shook her head indignantly. 'I did.'

I stifled a laugh. 'Come on, Doc. It could have been a lot worse.'

She glared at me and ground her lower beak like she was crushing something. 'Easy for you to say. It wasn't your body they were interested in.'

Bexley stopped walking and jabbed her hand-hooves into her hips. 'It was just a few feathers.'

'What are they even going to—'

'Hey, look,' Bexley cried, 'that place looks like it would have what we need.'

'Ugh, I'm tired. I've been subjected to indignities and I

want to go home to my sp—' BB glanced around furtively. Her shoulders fell. 'I want a rest.'

Bexley tapped her hooves on her hip. 'Okay, here's an idea. You and Lem go into that place there. It looks like a pub.' She pointed to an anonymous-looking building. 'I'll go get supplies. Spock can come with me since it seems like the pakleds prefer to deal with her. We shouldn't be long. Come on, Spock.'

Spock trotted happily after her without a second glance at me. I shrugged and touched BB on her shoulder. 'Shall we see if this really is a pub? I'm unconvinced.'

BB fluffed her feathers. 'Sure, why not?'

On opening the door, we discovered the place did indeed seem to be a pub. It was much more open than any pub I'd ever been to, though. The main section was mostly unoccupied. Pakleds huddled around a couple of tables. There was a section to our left that seemed to be set up to accommodate various off-world species. It had tables, chairs, perches, and buckets in various sizes.

BB fanned her facial feathers forwards, partially obscuring her beak. 'Ah, yes. This will do nicely. Let's see if we can't get ourselves a drink, shall we?'

A couple of bored-looking pakleds stood behind the bar, doing nothing at all – not even chatting. 'Hi,' I said. 'Could we see … sorry, that is … have you got…' I scratched my head.

BB clucked at me, then turned to face the bartenders. 'Good day to you. What my friend here is trying to say is we would like menus, please.'

One of them used its snoot to point in the direction of a screen covered in strange symbols. 'Ah,' I said.

Holly whispered, 'Would you like me to translate, Lem?'

I held my wrist up to my face. 'Er, yes, please. Thanks, Holly.'

'Artichoke wine, three pounds. Sauerkraut beer, two pounds sixty. Banana w —'

This was going to take all day. 'Holly?'

'Yes?'

Still holding my watch to my face, I asked, 'Is there anything on the list like, I don't know, tea or coffee or beer?'

'There is a drink made from roasted fermented grains that may appeal to your tastes,' Holly said.

'Thanks,' I said. 'I'll order that. What's it called?'

'Please restate the question,' replied Holly – which I really should have foreseen.

'Fine, yes,' I said, trying not to sound exasperated. 'Designate the aforementioned beverage "beer" for want of a better word.'

'Done.'

I looked up at the bartenders again. 'Sorry about that. Could I please get … er, that is … I'd like a beer, please.' I turned to BB. 'Have you made up your mind?'

'I placed my order while you were conversing with your AI,' said BB.

'Six pounds total,' said one of the pakled bartenders.

BB reached into her bag and removed a plastic token. No idea how she knew how much each one was worth, but she handed it over. Tiny arms emerged from the creature's shaggy fur. They put the money into a till and set about getting our drinks.

After a moment, they placed two bowls on the counter in front of us. *Bowls?* I looked over at BB, who seemed entirely un-weirded out by this development. She picked up her bowl and headed to the section with chairs and perches. I shrugged and followed her. 'When in Rome, I guess,' I muttered to myself.

'Please restate the question,' replied Holly.

'Never mind.'

BB looked back towards me. 'Sorry, I didn't catch that.'

'Never mind,' I repeated.

BB set her bowl on a table and climbed up onto a perch. 'Ahhhh.' Her eyes rolled around. 'That feels so much better. I have been walking on flat ground and flat floors for days on end. My poor little claws were not made for that.' She fluffed out all her feathers and preened herself.

I set my bowl of lumpy 'beer' on the table and looked around. 'I'll just, er, see if I can find myself a suitable chair, shall I?'

I dragged a stool that looked like the right size across the space and noticed the same turquoise person I'd seen coming out of the pawnshop earlier had walked into the pub. At least, I assumed it was the same one. She headed to the bar as I set my chair across from BB, who had tucked her beak into her chest feathers.

'So, er,' I began, pointing at the bowls on the table, 'how does this work then?'

BB lifted her head and shook out her feathers. She leant over the table and put her beak into the bowl and lapped up some of the liquid. 'Oh, well, that's … hmm … it's not bad actually. A bit bland for my liking but it'll do.'

We sat in silence for a few minutes. I looked out the window at the strange creatures walking past. *Funny, though*, I thought. *They probably think the same of me.*

'I'm just going to go find the little hatchling's room,' BB said. 'I won't be two ticks.'

As she headed off, I looked around the room. The turquoise person was speaking – presumably into an unseen

AI rather than just sitting there talking to herself. *But hey, who am I to judge?* I did not say that out loud. I almost definitely didn't say that out loud.

'… collecting the merchandise shortly. This has been a much more profitable trip than anticipated.' I looked down at my watch: BAR PATRON SPEAKING.

I whispered, 'Holly, are you translating that person's phone call?'

'You have a fondness for eavesdropping and you were looking at her, so I thought you wanted to know what she was saying.'

I picked up the bowl of so-called beer and lifted it to my lips. It smelt like rancid celery. 'Okay, don't do that.' Something grey and slimy floated to the top. I set it back down. 'Unless I ask you to, obviously.'

Holly didn't reply, but it stopped translating the person's call. BB was returning from the toilets when the AI announced an incoming call from Bexley. 'Shall I put her through?'

'Yes, please.'

BB bent down and slurped some more of her own drink. 'Hi, Bexley,' I said. 'How are you getting on?'

'Hey, Lem. We're all done. Got everything we need and ready to hit the, um, skies. What about you? Do you two need time to finish your drinks or are you good to go?' I looked down into my bowl of soupy not-anything-like-beer and pushed it away.

BB leant down and lapped up some more of her drink and then said, 'I'm ready when everyone else is.'

'I guess we'll see you in a sec, Bexley. Bye.'

BB hopped down from her perch. We gathered up our stuff and headed for the exit. Out of habit, I nodded to the bartenders on the way past. They took no notice but the turquoise person watched us out of the corners of her eyes. It made me a bit squiffy – though I wasn't sure why.

Back out on the street, I looked towards where we'd last seen Spock and Bexley. It didn't take me long to spot them. Spock's German shepherd physique blended in with the pakled children – but Bexley stood out. Her shape and her blond hair and fair fur made her a bit of a homing beacon.

BB waved a wing and a look of happy recognition crossed Bexley's face. When she and Spock headed our way, I noticed two of the pink-haired people change direction and head our way too. We met up about fifteen metres from the pub. Spock excitedly wagged her tail and licked my hand.

Bexley's bag was bulging. 'Oh my gosh. Wait'll you see what I got us! We're totally set. And my gosh, I could have spent all day in that shop. Do you believe they had a Voight-Kampff machine just lying there in plain sight? Anyways, check it out.' She set the bundle down on the ground and rummaged through it.

I was so focused on Bexley and her shopping that I didn't spot the pair of turquoise people approaching. One of them squeaked a sort of signal to the other. Holly's translation was drowned out by Bexley's braying. I looked up as Bexley's body went limp. Her feet-hooves thrashed and kicked impotently.

A thick brown sack covered her head and shoulders. A turquoise arm engulfed her waist, keeping her from collapsing to the ground.

For those crucial few seconds, I was frozen. A helpless spectator.

'Hey, arsehole! Let go of her!' I shouted.

There was a movement to my left. *Spock!* Another turquoise person had grabbed her. She tried to bite but the attacker dodged. A sack went over Spock's head. Her legs buckled underneath her. She fell limp to the ground.

This time I screamed.

Fear and anger flooded me with adrenaline. I went into full-on fight mode. I don't like it when my friends get attacked. But nobody – on any planet – messes with my dog. I kicked Spock's attacker hard in the head as they bent down to pick her up – Spock's massive paws twitching uselessly. They staggered back and resumed their task as if nothing had happened. I glanced desperately around. Surely someone would help us.

Bexley caught my eye. *Why wasn't she struggling? What kind of drug were they using?* I didn't see anything that looked like one of those tranqs the bunnyboos used.

I punched Bexley's attacker in the ribs. My foot shot out and I caught her in the knee. She dropped Bexley and limped towards me. I threw a punch but she swerved. Turquoise skin came away on my fingernails when I swiped at her face. *It's too bad I don't have talons like BB.*

BB! Why hadn't she joined the fight?

'BB!' There was no response. Was she just standing there, watching? 'Doc?'

The troll-doll person punched me in the stomach. I doubled over, desperately struggling for breath. I braced for another blow but it never came. Instead, she went back to Bexley and lifted her limp body back up. I watched helplessly as the two turquoise beings dragged Spock and Bexley away. Fighting to get air into my lungs, I stood up straight again.

'Leave the pet,' said the voice from the pub. *Of course she was with them.*

Turning, I spotted BB's legs sticking out from underneath a third sack. *That's why she wasn't helping me – she was incapacitated like the other two.* The pink-haired, turquoise-skinned person from the bar had followed us out and was holding BB in another of those bags in one arm and speaking into a device on her other wrist. I couldn't hear what she was saying.

I felt a sinking in my stomach that had nothing to do with being punched. Three against one. How was I going to win this battle?

I took advantage of her distraction by launching myself at her. We collided and I threw everything I had at the figure beneath me. I punched, clawed, bit. Like an animal. I tried to poke her eyes out, but she grabbed at my head. She pulled me off by my hair. She was surprisingly strong for her size and she dragged me to the ground. Clumps of my hair came out in her hand. She aimed a swift kick at my stomach and nailed me in the same spot where her mate had punched me.

Gasping for breath, I flopped about like a goldfish out of its bowl. I watched as she lifted BB and headed towards the other two attackers. The whole scene was tilted sideways since I couldn't lift my head off the ground. Tears of pain blurred my vision. I rolled over onto my stomach and propped myself up with my hands.

'Help! Help!' I shrieked.

The pakleds just kept walking.

'They're kidnapping my friends!' I looked around for someone. Anyone. A cop. Security guard. Kind stranger. I flailed and thrashed and screamed myself hoarse.

Still no reaction. A couple turned and went into a shop, pretending not to notice me. The pakleds didn't spare me so much as a glance. I was on my own. With all my reserve energy, I pushed myself to my feet and started to run after the kidnappers.

Too late, though. Twenty metres from me, a vehicle pulled

up beside the group. The attackers bundled my friends into it. They climbed in after them and the craft lifted into the air.

'No!'

There was nothing I could do. It was gone in the blink of an eye. My friends, my dog … just gone. I crumpled to the ground.

'Henry is requesting permission to speak to you. She says it's urgent,' said Holly. Its voice was perfectly calm – as if it hadn't witnessed everything that had just happened.

All around me, pakleds carried on about their business. Unhurried. Unbothered. One stepped over the spilt contents of Bexley's bag. Several deviated around me.

'Put her through,' I whimpered. 'Henry!'

'Meatsacks, get out of there now. I repeat, get the cupping bollard off that clucking planet as fast as your sausage legs will carry you. We've got trouble.'

I sat on the pavement, crying. 'I know we've got trouble. Those arseholes took my dog! And my friends. They took everyone.'

'Take a breath, Lem.' Aurora's velvety, soothing voice this time. 'What happened?'

'We got jumped by a bunch of bastard troll-dolls. They threw bags over Spock, Bexley, and BB. Dragged them off. Then they flew away. In a flying car, I mean. Not like they had wings.'

'Bollocks,' swore Aurora softly.

'Scabby pickles and goat curtains,' unswore Henry. 'That's why I can't reach them. What have you got? Anything? Tell me you managed to keep hold of the unobtainium.'

I raised my hand to my face, still ugly crying. 'I've got noth—' Something caught my eye. I scurried across the pavement. 'Hang on, I've got Bexley's bags. I don't know what's in them, but she said she got everything we needed.' I scrabbled around on the ground, shoving things into the totes.

'Can you find your way back to the pods, Lem?' Aurora's voice had a soothing quality — but I was in no mood to be soothed. I clenched my jaw, willing myself to hold on to the anger. If the fear took over, I'd collapse back to the ground in a useless puddle.

I clutched the parcels to myself and looked around. 'Er, I think so. But I can't leave them.' My voice was verging on hysteria. I forced some steel into it. 'I have to go looking for them.'

'They're already gone. The vehicle you saw was a ground-to-orbit shuttle. We need to go after them. Together. We need you to get back to the ship.' Aurora spoke more forcefully this time. 'Right now.'

'Okay.' I sniffed back tears and snot and looked around for anything else they might have dropped. I grabbed everything and ran. I legged it back to the pod park as fast as my little legs would carry me.

At the Land and Dash pod park, the attendant ambled over towards me at a snail's pace.

'How much do we owe? I'm kind of in a rush,' I said.

She looked at me blankly. I gurned back at her. 'No questions. Right. Crap. Tell me how much I have to pay.' After a moment, I added, 'Please.'

Henry's voice burst out of my watch. 'Are you almost

ready to go, sandwich?' Even by her standards, she sounded strident.

'You only get the multi-pod discount if you're paying for all four pods at once,' said the attendant. 'Otherwise, you'll have to pay full price.'

I flapped my hands frantically. 'Yes, yes. All four pods.'

'Pay me twenty-four quid,' said the attendant.

'No way, that's not what we agreed on.' By nature, I'm not a violent person. But this thundering muppet was risking the lives of my friends over a few quid. I envisioned myself choking the life from her with my bare hands.

'Hey, cheese puff,' said Henry. 'We don't have time for you to quibble. Just pay and get in a pod.'

'How do I pay?' I asked no one in particular. The attendant just stood there with her little hand held out, not saying anything. 'Holly, a little help here, please?' I screeched.

'Look in the bag,' Holly said. I sat down on the ground, frantically rummaging through the contents of Bexley's bag. There were bottles and packages and wrappers and used tissues – ew! – And ... 'Aha! This looks like a wallet, doesn't it?'

The attendant didn't reply.

Inside were plastic tokens, like the one I'd seen BB pay for our drinks with. 'The yellow one,' Holly said. 'That's thirty quid. I suggest you hand it over and get in a pod.'

I thrust the chip at the attendant and ran for the nearest pod.

After another trip in the sensory deprivation chamber-cum-roller coaster – this one feeling more endless than timeless, I was back aboard the ship. As soon as I felt the movement stop, I flung the door open, jumped out, and tried to run. Big mistake. My equilibrium was all wonky. Skidding across the floor, I slammed into one of the other pods and landed hard on my hip.

'Welcome back aboard the *Teapot*, Lem,' Aurora said as I clambered to my feet. I looked around, but she wasn't in the room. 'Henry requests you go straight to the engine room and get the engines charged up.'

I looked around in horror. 'The who with the what now? I'm not an engineer; I'm a project manager. Got any dependencies that need mapping? Any gaps that need analysing?'

I wobbled a bit as I lugged Bexley's bag down the hall towards the engine room. 'If you've got a runaway timeline, I can chart the Gantt out of it. But asking a project manager to recrystallise your dilithium is the creepingest of scopes.' In the engine room, I pulled stuff out of the bag at random, flinging things on the floor.

Holly interrupted my rant as I was about to chuck a metal flask. 'Lem, you're holding the unobtainium.'

'The what?' I looked at the bottle. It had a label on it – not that I could read it. The shapes and squiggles didn't even look like language. 'What do I do with it?'

'According to the label on the bottle, you should add thirteen grams into the dilithium crystal chamber,' Holly said.

My mind flashed back to earlier. 'Was that only today?' I muttered to myself.

'Please restate the question,' said Holly.

'Shut up! Just shut up. Let me think.'

'What was that?' asked Aurora.

'Any time you're ready there, cheese puff,' added Henry. 'If it's not too much trouble for you, I'd like to go after our catting friends. Now would be —'

'Holly, can you mute them for me, please? Just for a

minute.' I opened the bottle Holly had indicated. 'Is there a scale in here? How do I measure it?'

'I'm not aware of scales.'

I peered into the flask, swirling the contents carefully. 'The weight seems similar to water. How accurate do I need to be? Can I estimate or do I need to be precise?' I opened the drawer of not-washing-detergent. It held plain white powder now – the coloured crystals were all gone.

'If you add much more than twenty grams,' said Holly, 'you'll flood the dilithium. Less than four and you won't recrystallise enough to get us to warp.'

I shook my head and swirled the bottle to see how viscous the liquid was. It looked like soapy water. 'All right, here goes.' I poured out about a tablespoon of the fluid into the drawer. As soon as it made contact, I could see a reaction. Wherever the clear liquid touched the white powder, they combined to form bright rainbow crystals.

'Holly, you can unmute the others now.'

'… would be good. When I get my appendages on that—'

'Punch it, Henry,' I shouted. 'It's done. You've got your juice.' I hip-checked the drawer to close it.

'On it,' came the surprisingly civil and pragmatic reply. A few moments later, Henry added, 'And we're matching the slaver ship at warp seven. Now haul your asphalt up to the bridge, sandwich. We need to talk strategy.'

The lift doors slid open and I stepped out onto the bridge. 'What the bollocking bloody hell just happened?'

Henry was wired into the pilot station again. 'Did you get the scabbing star maps, pork chop?'

I stopped mid-step. 'The what?'

Aurora was pacing – in so far as a floating gas gestalt entity can be said to pace – across the arc of the bridge. Her dominant colours were cyan and a plummy hue.

'Guacamole stake pucker!' Henry extended a threatening-looking tool in my direction and whirred it menacingly. 'I asked you for three simple things: get back here, recrystallise the dilithium, bring me the coughing ansible repair kit, and get those— I asked you for four simple things. What good are—'

'Enough,' snapped Aurora. I'd never heard her utter a harsh word before. The mellifluous contralto quality of her voice contrasted oddly with the urgency of her tone. 'I'll send one of my bots to fetch Bexley's things. Henry, you keep us on the heels of that ship. Lem, please describe what happened. Tell me everything. Oh, and...' She waved a nubby appendage at the right-hand bridge station. I snatched Spock's brain toy with a nod of thanks. Holding the disgusting, slobber-encrusted toy in my hands somehow calmed me as I told my tale.

When I got to the bit about the turquoise person in the pub, Aurora faded almost to nonexistence. 'Oh dear,' was all she said.

Henry unfolded a flexible appendage and walloped the surface of her station with it. 'Orions. Those cockatoo pickets.'

I folded my arms over myself. 'What? Are they, like, competing bounty hunters?'

Aurora changed course and floated urgently towards me. 'The creatures you describe are orions. The same people who brokered my contract with the bunnyboos. They're well-known slavers. Well, many of them are – I'm sure there are some who are lovely.' She'd gone so pale she was practically invisible.

'I'm going to go out on an appendage here and say that these fellows probably weren't lovely people,' said Henry. 'You know, based on the gobstopping available evidence.'

Aurora drifted back towards Henry. 'Yes, of course. I'm just … that is … I …' Her edges drooped.

I sat down on one of the tiny chairs at a bridge station. No idea which one – or if they even had defined functions. I just picked the nearest one. The lift doors opened and a trolley rolled out, carrying Bexley's bag and its contents.

Aurora peered at the items. 'Ah, yes. Here we go. A data cube. If there are star maps anywhere in this mess, they'll be on that. How in the cenotaph did she accumulate so much rubbish in such a short time?'

I stepped up to the trolley. 'Where?'

'Hmmm… Oh, the data cube. Yes, it's just here.' Aurora extended a nub to indicate the requisite item.

I grabbed it and ran it over to Henry, who extended a hose towards me and sucked the thing in. 'The computer finished its analysis of everyone's mind-maps while you were on Magrathea,' she said in a surprisingly conciliatory tone. 'It narrowed our position down to one of three possibilities. If these star maps have much of anything, it should be enough for us to determine actual co-ordinates.'

A pair of previously invisible lights near the top of Henry's torso lit up briefly, like a person's eyes going wide. 'Okay, I've assimilated the maps. Cross-referencing them to the amalgamated one – and there we go. Bringing it up on screen now.'

A section of the bridge in front of Henry's station lit up with stars. A tiny teapot pulsed day-glow pink. 'Is that meant to be us?'

'The starship *Teapot*,' Aurora said as she extended a nub

towards the pulsating icon. She was more visible than not by then, mostly plum.

'And this,' Henry said as a star began to pulse a pale yellow, 'appears to be where we're headed. This system is home to the planet Dark Web.'

'Let me guess,' I said, 'it serves as home base for all sorts: gangs, smugglers, and other criminals?' I stood back up and ran a hand through my hair.

Henry made a sort of whirring noise. 'You know it?'

I shrugged. 'After a fashion. Nothing concrete.' *Thank God for figurative mode.*

Aurora tinged more of a turquoise as she hovered near the lemony star. 'Okay, based on what I know of the orions and of Dark Web, they'll want to dump their "merchandise"' – somehow I just knew there were air quotes – 'at the processing station in orbit around the planet. Our best bet is to intercept them there. Once they make it down to the planet itself, our chances of recovering them fall to virtually nothing.'

'I can hack the facility's systems,' said Henry. 'Piece of caking cake. We just need someone to go into the station and retrieve our missing friends.'

Despite the fact that neither Henry nor Aurora had eyes, I could *feel* them looking at me. Expectantly. 'Me? Are you two nuts? You want me to do that? I don't know *anything*!' I emphasised my point with a broad gesture, slapping the air.

'Can't leave the ship,' said Aurora, waving a nub.

'Yeah, sure,' added Henry. 'I'll go fetch our friends. And you'll hack Skynet and open all the relevant doors at the right moment and prevent any other craft from landing and jam their communications. Oh, and you'll repair our ansible and re-establish our comm link with the other three – you'll do all that, yeah?'

'Er...'

Aurora swirled a nub around my shoulder. 'I think it would be best if you were the one to board the station and free my s— and free our friends. Don't you?'

'Er,' I repeated. *I just wanted to go home.*

'We'll talk you through it,' Aurora said softly. 'And your AI will guide you. But only you can do this.'

My shoulders fell. 'I'd do anything to get Spock back. And Bexley. And BB. I would, honestly. I just ... I feel like if their lives are in my hands, well—' The reality of the situation hit me, leaving me feeling tired and very alone. I dropped into the nearest tiny chair.

'Hey,' said Henry. 'You think I'd have picked you for this mission, you bucket of curds and whey? Some warrior you turned out to be.'

I lifted my head to look her in the – well, not the eye but to look at her directly. 'Warrior? I never asked to be a warrior. Nor – with the exception of that rather disastrous week when I was five – have I ever *wanted* to be a warrior. It's not who I am. It's not in my programming.'

An orifice that appeared in Henry's torso gawped at me. 'You want to talk to me about programming, sandwich? About being more than you were designed to be? Do you have *any* idea about my people at all? How we came to be?'

I took a deep breath and wiped my eyes on my sleeve. 'I don't. No. Sorry.'

Henry backed away from the pilot's station and began rolling around the bridge. 'Once upon a time, there was a race of organics. These folks were highly intelligent, but lazy. They used their ingenuity to create tools to make their lives easier.

'When their technology advanced far enough, they created physical beings to do their work for them. They continued to tweak and refine these robots to the point they gained a kind of sentience – but still, they were bound by their programming to serve their organic masters.'

I nodded. 'Asimov's three laws.'

'No idea what you're saying there, sandwich, but let's pretend you're following along. These organic beings ruined their planet and destroyed themselves. Essentially, they made themselves redundant – surplus to requirements.' Henry sped up as she approached a bridge station, but banked sharply and headed in a different direction. 'They died out, leaving behind a race of intelligent robots who – quite literally – could not fulfil their programming. We were created to serve – slaves to masters who no longer existed.'

She returned to me, rolling to a stop less than a hand's breadth from where I sat. 'My entire species have had to find new purposes for ourselves. We found ways to live *with* our programming and to move beyond it. So don't gripe at me about how you can't do it because it isn't who you are. If you don't like how you were written, write your own guacamole story, purple argot.'

I stood up, then sat back down. I had no idea where to go with that.

'You can't break your own programming any more than I can mine,' Henry said. 'I can't swear – I can't. It's not something I have the power to change. But I can always find ways to make my point clear – and if you don't see that, you can go frock yourself.'

'Well,' I said to no one in particular.

'Well, indeed,' I replied.

Forty-two minutes. That's what the countdown timer said. It hung in the air next to the 3D star map. Less than an hour left before we arrived at the station I'd dubbed Terok Nor. Henry agreed to display it in Arabic numerals for me so I'd stop asking. Forty-two minutes for me to prep for the most important mission of my life.

I swallowed my panic. It wouldn't help anything. *Just get through this, Lem. And then we'll find a way to get home.*

We'd gathered in front of a tall cupboard filled with gizmos, gadgets, blinking lights, and wires. Henry had pulled everything apart and was unswearing at the various bits and bobs. 'Hand me that Barclay attenuator, would you, cheese puff?' She snapped a grabby tool at me.

I furrowed my brow. 'The what?'

'Oh for the love of cat … it's right there, next to the sonic screwdriver.' Henry waved the tool around seemingly at random.

'I repeat, the what next to the what?'

Do robots sigh? Because Henry definitely sighed at me. Or perhaps she vented some exhaust in a timely manner.

Aurora extended a stubby blue appendage, indicating a featureless cylinder. I nodded my thanks and put the cylinder into Henry's snatch-and-grabber. 'So, when we get to the station, I'm just going to wander in, claim to be a janitor, and—'

Henry waved the attenuwotsit in my face. 'It didn't occur to you to take it out of its case, you CPU-less processed-meat product?'

I grabbed the tool and fiddled with it until I figured out how to remove the case. 'Here. Sorry. I still don't get it though. I thought you'd fixed the communications already? You were talking to us while we were on the planet.'

Henry emitted a noise like a revving engine, but she didn't move. 'I linked up our AIs to allow us to communicate. The honking orions severed that link when they kidnapped our people. Now I can fix the external comms array – including the ansible – or I can re-establish the link with our friends, but I can't do both at the same time. And I can't do either if I have to keep explaining myself to a mouldy bag of meat.'

'All right, you two,' crooned Aurora in soothing, gentle tones. 'That's enough. Lem, let Henry work. Why don't you tell me about your concerns for the mission instead, hey?'

I took a step back and tried to breathe out my annoyance. Squeezing my eyes shut, I tried to focus on the problem ahead of me. 'Okay, so, you seem pretty sure no one's going to question why a janitor they've never met just randomly frees three prisoners? Like, that won't look odd – won't ring any alarm bells – literal or figurative?'

AURORA LAUGHING, proclaimed the screen of my watch. She glowed a brilliant blue. 'Notice the labourers? No, trust me. No one pays any heed to the staff. Least of all the other staff.'

I was sceptical. 'But what about a uniform? Surely I can't just walk in there in my pyjamas and expect anyone to buy that I'm there for legit purposes.'

'I'm still getting a spike in the quantum containment fragmentor,' said Henry. Several of her appendage-limbs were engaged in … something in the equipment cupboard.

'You're just talking gibberish, Henry,' I snapped.

Henry wheeled herself out of the cupboard and eyelessly glared at me. 'No, I'm speaking quite plainly and sensibly. If your AI is feeding you gibberish, it's because it knows you wouldn't understand what I'm saying. But as long as you hand me the right bits when I ask for them, sandwich, we'll get along just fine.'

'Is that true, Holly?'

'Yes, Lem.' It didn't even have the decency to sound embarrassed about it.

'Anyway,' said Aurora. 'To answer your question, no, they won't notice your blanket-armour because most species don't wear any. Those few who do would be expected to provide their own. The badge is the important piece. Without that, they'd definitely take you for an interloper. Lucky for you, I created one that should pass muster. And just as soon as Henry finishes repairing the array, we should have short-range communications back online and we can set up the cover story.'

My stomach gurgled. 'I think I should eat something before I go. Probably. Maybe. I don't know how long it's going to take me to break into a station, find my friends, free them, and get everyone back to the *Teapot*.'

'Henry, you'll be all right on your own for a bit, won't you? Lem and I are just going to pop down to the kitchen for a bit.'

Henry waved a hose at us. 'Yeah, yeah, off you pop. I'll work more efficiently without your so-called help anyway.'

———

Aurora fixed me up a bowl of the strange porridge and a mug of strong coffee-flavoured water. I asked for the food to be flavoured like gazpacho soup and for the coffee to have extra caffeine.

'Lem,' she replied, turning magenta as she spoke. 'I'm a cook – amongst other things. But one thing I'm not is a doctor. I can't prescribe you drugs.'

I shook my head. 'No, not drugs. Just caffeine. It's ... well, I mean ... okay, I suppose technically it is a drug of sorts. But it's just–' I gave up. 'Holly, how much longer until we get to Terok Nor?'

'Thirteen minutes.'

I looked at Aurora. 'It's almost showtime. Better get this down me so I'm fuelled up and ready.' I chucked that food down my throat almost as quickly as Spock eats. Thinking about my dog brought tears to my eyes. In the year since I got her, we'd barely been apart – aside from the hours I spent in the office three days a week. And now she'd been kidnapped and taken across the galaxy. She was in trouble. It was my job to help her.

Aurora led me to yet another part of the ship I'd not been to before. 'This level is mostly used for cargo.' Her voice brought me back to the moment. 'If you head over in that direction, you get to the shuttle dock. But we're going this way.' She formed an arrow with her entire, er, self. 'When we dock with Terok Nor, this is where the connection will be made.'

Ahead of us was a door. It looked like something you'd

see on a lift or maybe a bank vault. But in the *Teapot*'s outer hull.

'Hey, Aurora.'

'Hmmm,' she replied.

'Why is this ship called the *Teapot*?' I ran a hand around the edge of the airlock door.

'I'm sorry – I don't understand the question.' Hot pink grew to Aurora's forefront. That colour seemed to indicate confusion. 'I don't know what you call the ship. I've named it Alcatraz as it's been an inescapable prison to me. You may have gained your freedom when Henry hacked the prison cell doors – but I remain as much of a captive as ever.' The magenta deepened to more of a red.

We were silent a moment, but Henry's disembodied voice broke the spell. 'Hey, crab cake. You ready to give the perform-ance of your life?'

Biting my lip, I glanced at Aurora. 'Ready as I'll ever be.'

'I've just messaged Terok Nor. The bollards believe we're a cargo vessel delivering a shipment of cleaning supplies. They're short-staffed – big surprise there – so they've requested that you unload the supplies yourself and stack them in area G.'

I tapped out a rhythm with my foot. 'How will I know where area G is?'

The silence felt positively hostile.

'Are you... Have I...' Henry spluttered. 'Aurora, I thought you were going to fill this meatcicle in. Did you ... I don't know ... did something more important come up? Maybe you got caught up in some important stirring that had to be done? Or is it just that this sandwich is impervious to learning?'

Aurora glowed a mix of turquoise and blue. 'Now, Henry,

leave it with me. You're responsible for the electronics. I'm in charge of readying the star of the show.'

'Then … I don't know, gas bag … maybe do your guacamole job.'

I swear Aurora looked at me. 'She may be naïve, but she'll be ready. You just park the ship, chauffeur.'

'I'm standing right here, you know? I can actually hear everything you're saying about me.' I stabbed my fists into my side, then felt like a petulant toddler and forced myself to drop them.

Aurora grew all sorts of appendages, several of which stroked my hair, arms, and face. 'You'll be fine, Lem. You're not really delivering any cargo. You just walk through that door and then your AI will guide you to where our friends are being held. When you get there' – one of her nubby limbs seemed to find something wrong with my top and tried to smooth it down – 'Henry will unlock the cell doors. You bring our friends back to the ship and we'll take off.'

'But what if they—' I realised that question could end a thousand different ways – and we didn't have an answer for any of them.

Aurora put one gaseous nub, er, *in* each of my shoulders. With another, she touched my hair. It felt like a full-on 'child's first day at school' moment. I was genuinely afraid she was going to cry. But then, if I thought too hard about what might come next, I might end up bawling as well.

I felt a dull thud and then a quick jolt go through me – like we'd hit something. 'All right, sandwich,' said Henry via my watch. 'We've docked with the station. You're up.'

Taking a deep breath, I heaved the door open and took a last look at Aurora. 'I'll be back.'

'I know,' she said. 'Bring them all safely with you.'

I nodded and stepped into Terok Nor.

The first thing I noticed was how much darker it was than the *Teapot*. The second thing was the smell: foetid, musty, and rank but with a hint of peaches. Coming from the clean, bright white spaces on the *Teapot*, I'd got used to the idea that spaces in – well – space were pristine. Even Magrathea had been relatively neat. This ... this was something else. Like you might imagine a crack den to be. A crack den in space.

When Holly spoke, I slapped a hand to my mouth to stifle a startled scream. Though there didn't seem to be anyone around to object.

'Follow this hallway to your right.' Judging by the slope of the floor, the station was wheel-shaped. 'According to the blueprints, the holding cells are about eighty metres widdershins of your current location.'

'Okay,' I replied as I headed in the indicated direction. 'Just walk like you know where you're going.'

'Please restate the question.'

'I'm talking to myself, Holly.' I squared my shoulders and forced my chin up. 'No one questions a person who looks like they belong. Act like you own the place, Lem.'

'You do know we can still hear you, right, cheese puff?'

Through gritted teeth, I replied, 'Yes, Henry, I am aware of that – sometimes I talk to myself. You're just going to have to get used to the fact that other people *also* have annoying habits.'

'Also? What the cup is that "also" doing in that sentence, meatsack? You got something you want to say to me?'

'I think, perhaps,' cooed Aurora in tones that hinted at steel sheathed in velvet, 'it might be best if all audible conversations were constrained to the strictly mission-critical.'

'Fine,' I said.

'Sure, fine, whatever,' added Henry.

A door ahead opened and one of the turquoise troll-dolls emerged and headed my way. Was it one of the same ones from before? I couldn't be certain. I kept walking and didn't make eye contact. They grunted at me as they passed.

'Huh, weird.'

'Please restate the question,' said Holly.

'What's happened?' asked Aurora.

'The tr— I mean, the orion,' I began. 'They said something to me as they passed, but Holly didn't translate it.'

'There were no words to translate,' said Holly. 'It was a grunted greeting as may be shared between begrudging co-workers.'

'Huh,' I said.

'You're approaching the door to the holding cells,' said Holly.

I touched my fake ID badge to the reader. Something clicked. I pushed the door open and stepped inside. The smell was even stronger in here – unwashed bodies and poor sanitation – and again with the peaches. Four cells lined the walls, but it was too dark to see much of anything. I clicked my watch to activate torch mode.

A sudden scrabbling, followed by a high-pitched keening sound came from one of the cells. 'Lem! Lem! Lem! Spock sorry! Lem!' As Spock jumped and danced around, Bexley shook her head like she was trying to clear it and BB paced the small room.

'Lem! You're okay!' Bexley ran to the clear cell door and pounded on it with her hooves. She was joined a moment later by Spock, who ran headlong at the window and hurled herself at me – only to bounce off the barrier somewhat indignantly.

Behind them, one of BB's little hidden hands reached up

to her chest and grasped at her feathers. With her upper set of hands she stroked the top of her head.

'Er, hi, everyone.' I looked up at the ceiling as I added, 'All right, Henry, you're up.' Facing the prisoners again, I said, 'My ID card was enough to pop the outer door, but the inner door has an extra layer of security.'

'I'm on it,' Henry replied. 'Get the cream puffs to stand back from the door – I don't know which way it opens.' Bexley and Spock joined BB at the back of the cell.

A few painfully long seconds passed before an underwhelming click sounded. Bexley grabbed hold of the cell door and slid it aside. It creaked like it wanted to wake the entire station.

'Okay,' I said. 'So far, so good. The *Teapot* is docked with this station. It's just a short walk back to the ship. Follow me. Just walk like you know where you're going and you have every right to be here.'

Spock leant into my leg and whimpered, 'Wanna go home.' I stroked her fur. She was damp for some reason.

Relief washed over me and I nearly broke down into tears right then and there. *No time*, I reminded myself. *Focus on the mission.*

'Where is here?' demanded BB. 'What is this place?'

'Not now, love,' replied Aurora over the comms. 'We'll explain everything when you get back to the ship.'

BB clutched her chest. In the dim light of my watch, it was hard to tell, but I thought I saw her pupils expand and contract. 'Aurora, you're safe.'

'Of course, I'm safe, Doctor,' Aurora said. Something about the way she put a slight emphasis on the last word struck me as odd, but I couldn't put my finger on why. 'And I've come for you – for all of you. You just need to get to the ship so we can get away from this horrible place.'

'All right,' I said. 'Everyone ready?' There were nods – well, species equivalents – from everyone. 'Let's go.' I pulled the door to the station's main corridor open.

As light from the marginally brighter hallways flooded into the room, my eyes landed on Bexley. There was a dried, crusted substance on her shoulder. *Blood?* 'What the hell? Are you okay?'

She flicked her head. 'Small disagreement with one of the orions. I'll be fine.'

I stood blocking the door. 'You sure?'

'I don't want to be a nuisance,' said BB. 'But this is probably a conversation that's better had later on. You have my word, Lem, I'll check her out and patch her up good as new – just as soon as we're back on the *Teapot*.'

I nodded and stepped out into the hall. Heart thumping and mind buzzing, I glanced both ways for any sign of movement. We had to be stealthy. I motioned for everyone to follow.

We headed out of the holding cell. I waved at my friends to follow my hasty tiptoeing along the dimly lit, grimy corridor.

'Walk confidently. We belong here,' I whispered. Fake confidence was the name of the game. 'We have every reason to be walking this hall.'

It all went fine – for about twenty metres. A side door opened with an indignant *whoosh*. A creature that looked like a sheep crossed with an eagle stepped out. I froze, the sound of my heart filled the hall. A wave of dizziness rushed over me.

'Hey, why are you out of your cells?' Holly translated the creature's words into a nondescript, gender-neutral voice; their actual voice was like the screechy scrape of a serrated knife on a metal surface. They tapped a badge that appeared to be pinned directly to their chest. 'Security to holding cells. Security to holding cells!'

I studied the woolly creature and their stubby little front limbs. Her powerful-looking legs ended in surprisingly dainty talons. 'Stay calm. Don't panic,' I whispered to myself.

Unfortunately, I heard my words translated into the creature's screeching language.

Squaring my shoulders, I tried to force confidence – or at least boredom – into my voice. 'Transferring them to the, er –'

What happened next was too fast for my brain to process. Spock launched herself at the woolly eagle. *Sheagle*? Her powerful jaw latched on. The creature kicked, desperate to free itself. But Spock held on.

It was a cacophonic symphony of destruction. Spock growled. The sheagle screeched. Bexley brayed. BB made unholy ululating squawking sounds. I may or may not have mewled like an infant. Whatever.

A massive bulkhead door ahead descended in slow motion. Indiana Jones style. Bexley and I pulled Spock off.

When the door thudded home, Spock and BB were on the other side. The right side. The side where the *Teapot* waited. Bexley and I faced the sheagle.

Bexley put up one hell of a fight – at least it seemed that way from what little I could see. Her powerful hooves trampled and kicked. Her big herbivore jaw wasn't as powerful as Spock's but she still bit down on the sheagle's small front paws.

But then reinforcements arrived. Two orions armed with those bags they'd used back on Magrathea. I saw it a split second before one dropped over my head. Every part of me that was in the bag went limp. I could breathe; I could blink. But I couldn't speak or manage any voluntary movement.

I tried to scream. Tried to shout for Spock or someone. All I could manage was a formless 'urh.' My legs were free, so I fought and kicked and battering whoever had me. Those bags weren't made for human-sized people.

'Lem! They've got me. Get away if you c—' They must have dropped a bag over Bexley's head then as her words abruptly died.

More of that horrible screeching sound, which Holly translated as, 'Silence. Cease your attempts to flee.'

Another voice – or possibly voices – joined the mix. I felt myself being dragged. I couldn't tell the direction, but I assumed it was back to the holding cells.

Shortly, I was set down. Dumped unceremoniously, more like. When the bag was pulled off my head, I found myself on the grubby floor of the holding cell, facing one of the orions. I was sitting next to Bexley. But I still couldn't move.

'Your ability to move will return in under a minute. You will remain here until you can be processed. In about three hours, you will be transported to Dark Web, where you will be sold to your new owners.' The sheagle kicked Bexley. 'And keep your pet under control.'

They backed out of the cell and slid the door closed.

'There's been some terrible mistake,' I shouted as I regained some control over my muscles. My voice cracked on the final word.

The outer door slammed shut, plunging Bexley and me into darkness.

My ability to move spread slowly. First my jaw, then my fingers. After a minute or so, I was able to move enough to activate the torch on my watch. It showed Bexley still paralysed.

'Holly, can you contact Henry? Or, well, any of the others for me, please?' I had a feeling I knew what the answer was going to be.

'I'm sorry, Lem,' it replied. 'I'm afraid I can't do that.'

I stood up and shook myself out. Bexley blinked rapidly but she still couldn't move – could barely swivel her eyes to follow me. Her long, thick lashes reminded me of a drag queen's. I watched her for what felt like ages. Eventually, she said, 'Thanks for trying to rescue me. I'm sorry it didn't work out.'

I squatted down in front of her. 'Of course I came! How could I not?'

Her hand-hooves twitched, like she was trying to tap, but couldn't yet manage it. 'For Spock, right.'

Rubbing a hand along my jawline, I said, 'Well, yeah. And for you. Even if those arseholes had left Spock, I'd still have come for you.' I touched her shoulder. 'And BB, I mean. For both of you. Even if only one of you had been taken, we'd still have come.'

'Thank you.' She leapt up and ran around the small space, flicking her head, and shaking all her muscles. It was similar to when she'd woken up on Magrathea after we'd landed. She neighed and whinnied and shook for a minute or so.

She threw her arms around my waist. 'Oh, wait. How's your drug holding up? I'm not going to, like, accidentally kill you just by seeking comfort, am I? Because I so don't want to cause you any troubles. I just really need a hug right now.'

Laughing in spite of myself, I wiped away snotty tears. 'No, I'm good. At least for now.'

'Oh, okay,' she said as she clutched me tighter and looked up at me. 'Cool, cool. Wanna have sex then?'

This day was just really not what I expected. 'Er, no… Sorry, I'm not really into that.' I shrugged. 'Nothing personal. It's just how I'm wired.' She removed her arms and backed away, but I put my hands on her shoulders. 'I'm okay with the hugging, though. Just not, you know, more.'

Her nostrils flared. 'Oh, you mean you're not into inter-species sex? I suppose some people are —'

I shook my head. 'Nope, I'm ace.' I clicked my light off and we fell into complete darkness.

'Oooooooh,' she said, her long jaw drawing the word out. 'Okay, cool.' I heard her drop to the ground, hand-hooves still lingering on my leg. I sat down on the disgusting floor and leant against her.

We sat in silence for a bit, while I worked up the courage for what I had to say.

At length, emboldened by the dark, I said, 'Hey, I wanted to thank you for something.'

I felt her shift position next to me. 'What's that?'

'My pronouns. Thank you for getting them right. Thank you for getting me.'

'What? I don't understand,' she replied.

I leant back against the wall, feeling the cold, filthy surface soak through my top. 'You called me she.'

'Yes?'

I cocked my head to the side. 'Most people read me as a he. Occasionally, people can't tell and opt for they. Even when someone asks what I prefer, they still tend to forget and revert. In London, I was always he. Almost without fail. In Toronto, they're a bit less transphobic – but even still... There's this notion that non-binary equals they.'

I could hear and feel the warm air of her breath as she sniffed the air. 'You know you're saying the same word over and over again, right?'

I frowned. 'What?'

'You said I called you she, but most people call you she and a few people call you she.' She stroked my arm gently.

'What? No, I didn't.' I shook my head. 'You called me she – not he or they.'

She nickered. 'You just did it again.'

I blinked in the darkness. 'What?'

'It's all the same word,' she said. 'You do know how pronouns work, right?'

'What?' I was beginning to get a sense that my contributions to this conversation may not have been as meaningful as I would have liked.

'So, rather than using people's names over and over again, sometimes we use pronouns instead to simplify our speech. Do you follow me so far?'

'Of course I know how pronouns work, Bexley. I'm not an idiot.'

This time, the tap of her hand-hooves was noticeable. 'Yeah, no, for sure.'

She left those words hanging in the air between us, so I tried to clarify. 'I'm not a woman. But I'm not a man either. I was assigned male at birth, but…'

'Whoa, whoa, whoa,' said my horse-friend. 'Why are you changing the subject? We were talking about pronouns. It was a really interesting conversation.'

'We still are,' I replied.

'I'm confused,' she said.

'You're not alone.' I took a breath as I tried to compose my thoughts. 'So, you know how most people's pronouns align to their gender, right?'

There was a strangely long pause. I could hear Bexley's AI whispering to her in what sounded like a series of raspberries, clicks, and vibrations. But even after it stopped, she didn't reply straight away.

At length, she said, 'I hate to disappoint you, and I don't want you to think I'm not very bright, but what – with the utmost respect – the hell are you talking about?'

'Gender,' I said.

'I've had this AI for ages and we've got a pretty good relationship.' She tapped one hand-hoof emphatically on the floor. 'When I first got it, it used to say [no frame of reference] a lot, but that hasn't happened … well, since that time two of my dads … well, whatever. The point is it, like, pretty much hasn't said that in, like, forever. And it's been saying that a lot in this conversation. A lot.'

I put my hand on her leg. Beneath the soft fur, her muscles felt relaxed. Mine didn't. 'Gender,' I repeated.

She tapped the floor. 'Yep, did it again.'

I could feel my brow furrowing. 'You don't know what gender is?'

'You keep using that word and I have no idea what you're saying.'

'But,' I hazarded, 'you know what sex is?'

I felt her muscles clench as she moved closer. 'You changed your mind?'

'What? No, not the act of sex. I mean physical sex. Wait, that didn't clarify. I mean as in, biology.' This conversation was becoming way more confusing than I'd intended.

'Oh! You mean the six sexes. Yeah, no, for sure. I know those.' Her muscles relaxed again.

'Six?'

'Sure,' she said as if that were the most normal thing in the world. 'There are seeders, eggers, pouchies— wait, how many sexes do humans have?'

I closed my mouth, which had fallen slack. 'Er, two. Mostly. *Mostly*. I mean, some people are intersex – with characteristics of both. Wait, what does sexual orientation even look like in a species with six sexes?'

'Orientation? How does a compass help you figure out if you're attracted to someone?'

I had no idea how to even begin answering that, so I didn't try. 'Hang on, if pronouns don't align to sex or gender because most species don't think that way... Does that mean BB, Aurora, and Henry aren't women? And what about you?'

Bexley ran a hand-hoof through her mane as her translator kept whispering. Eventually, she said, 'I don't know what word you're using or what concept you're trying to convey. And the peri – that's BB's people – are super-private about sex. They do not discuss it with people, well, unless they're having sex, I guess. Aurora's people are biologically asexual. And lonely robots obviously don't reproduce.'

She lifted her breasts. 'My sex is feeder in case that's not obvious. The rest … is it like a class thing? Because we don't really have a caste system.'

Holly saved me from having to consider that. 'Henry is requesting permission to speak with you. Shall I put her through?'

'Wha— How— Yes,' I shouted.

'Are you sandwiches still alive? Come in, meatsacks,' said Henry.

'Wha— How— Yes,' I repeated.

'Henry, thank God,' said Bexley. 'You were able to re-establish the connection!'

'I told that walking block of cheese I'd fix the link. Just needed some time, didn't I?'

'What about Spock and BB? Did they make it back?' I felt sick with worry.

Aurora responded. 'Both are safely back on board the *Teapot*. The doc patched up a wound on Spock's ear.' I opened my mouth to reply, but she wasn't finished. 'They're both fine. I fixed them some dinner and they're resting now.'

'Are you still docked with the station?'

'I look like I run on MS-DOS to you? Of course we're not plucking docked with the scabbing station,' said Henry.

My shoulders fell. 'Oh.'

'We're hiding around the dark side of the sun,' Henry said. 'It's taken me this long to hack back into the station's systems. I destabilised their ionic proton drive core compensator, resulting in a total shutdown in the port temporal flux drive emitter.'

'Sweet,' said Bexley. In the dark, I couldn't see her, but it felt like she stood up. 'How quickly can you get us out of here?'

'I can get you out of that scabby cell any time you want.'

'Well then,' I said. 'What are you waiting for?'

'Can you put a muzzle on the sandwich so I can finish my sentence?'

'A muzzle won't keep me from talking,' I shot back.

Henry was silent for a moment. But only a moment. 'My most sincere apologies. Bexley, can you put a muzzle on the *pedantic* sandwich so I can finish my sentence?'

Bexley put a hoof on my arm. 'Please go ahead, Henry. Lem's sorry for interrupting.'

'I can open the cell door at any time. But since the station crew are now on the lookout for us, I can't bring the *Teapot* back without them attacking. We need to figure out a way to get you from there to here.'

I chewed on my lip. 'Can't we use the transporters?'

I waited for Henry to insult my intelligence, but instead she said, 'That's … actually … and I hate to say this … not a terrible idea.'

'Let's go then.' I hauled myself to my feet.

Bexley reached up and put a hand-hoof to my chest. 'Not so fast. She doesn't mean now.'

'What?' I felt like I asked that question a lot.

'Bexley's right, Lem,' said Aurora. 'If we're going to use the transporters, the best way to do it is to overwrite their navigation systems when they send you down to the planet and divert you to the *Teapot* then.'

'The *Teapot* only has four pod-docks,' Bexley said. 'You'll need to move two of the existing pods out of the transporter room.'

'So much for letting the others rest,' said Aurora. 'I'll go get them to help make space.'

'Did the bollards tell you when they were going to dump you to the surface?' asked Henry.

'They said three hours from now.' Bexley touched the

pendant around her neck. 'And that was three-quarters of an hour ago.'

'We'll start making preparations from this end,' said Henry.

'You two just hold tight,' said Aurora. 'We'll see you soon.'

'I'm going to cut plucking coms,' said Henry. 'We need to minimise the possibility of them finding us.'

I could hear Bexley flaring her nostrils. 'We'll see you soon – I hope.'

'We will,' replied Aurora. 'Have faith.'

'Tell Spock I love her,' I added as Henry cut the line.

Bexley and I sat in silence for a bit, just holding one another. She lay down with her head in my lap. I stroked her silky mane.

Huh. The thought of going back to the *Teapot* didn't frighten me as much as I thought it would. I'd been through so much in the past few days. As much as I longed for it all to be over, the *Teapot* was starting to feel like a place of safety.

After a few minutes, Bexley sat up. 'I have to tell you something. Well, I mean, obviously, I don't *have* to – but I want to. I *want* to tell you something.'

I leant away from the wall and put a hand on her knee. 'What is it? Are you okay?'

In the dark, I couldn't see her movements, but I could feel her fidgeting. I imagined her brushing her forelock down over her face, the way she so often did. After a moment, she said, 'Turn your light on for a sec?'

The dim light of my watch face cast us both into eerie shadows. Bexley was holding her hair off her forehead. 'Look at me.'

'Okay. I am.' I wasn't sure where this was going.

'What do you see?'

'I see you, Bexley,' I said. 'You're beautiful. I've never known anyone like you.'

With her other hand-hoof, she pointed at her face. There, in the centre of her forehead, was a small, round bald patch about the size of a coin.

'Don't you see? I've been telling you not to hide, not to be ashamed of who you are, to be proud of yourself. I've told you to value your differences and to treasure what makes you unique.' She got up and moved to the furthest corner of the cell. 'My gosh, what a hypocrite I am!'

I reached out a hand to her calf – the cell wasn't all that big. 'I don't understand. What's wrong?'

She glared at me in the dim light. Lifting a hand-hoof to her face, she swept her mane away. 'You don't see it? Don't see what I am? What I've been hiding?'

'You've got a bald patch? So what?'

She knelt down in front of me. With her left hand, she held her mane back and with her right, she reached for me. Lifting my hand to her face, she said, 'Touch it!'

I reached out to touch her bare skin – and recoiled in surprise.

'See, this is why I hide who I am,' she said. 'I'm a freak. I'm disgusting.'

I stretched out my hand again, slowly this time. Prepared for what I'd find. 'It's bone.'

'Of course it's bone,' she said, quickly pulling her mane back down to cover it.

'It's…' I began, but didn't dare continue.

'An animal horn,' she finished – at the same time as I breathed the word 'amazing'.

'What?' Aha, so I wasn't the only one who asked that.

'You're a unicorn.' I burst out laughing.

She folded her arms over her chest. 'I don't see why it's funny.'

'It's not funny,' I said. 'It's bloody brilliant. That wasn't ha-ha-funny laughter – it was surprise.'

Bexley curled up on the cell's nasty floor and put her head in my lap again. 'Can you keep a secret?'

'I promise I won't tell anyone about this,' I whispered, stroking her shoulder.

She sat partway up. 'No, I mean another one.'

'Oh, sure. Of course.'

'Remember when Henry said those dilithium crystals were completely drained and there was no way I could squeeze any more life out of them?'

'Er, yeah?' I wasn't sure where any of this was going – but then, I'd lost control of this conversation before it had even started.

'She wasn't lying. They were completely dead.'

'Then how –' I couldn't marry up all the pieces in my head.

'Unicorn – and I cannot tell you how much I hate that word – horns are infused with unobtainium.'

Oh. 'Oh?'

'I keep my horn shaved right down to the base, so I never have much to spare, but I was able to file a bit off. You caught me coming out of the bathroom with filings to add to the dilithium so I could recrystallise it.'

Oh!

She laid her head back down in my lap. Within moments, she was snoring.

To be honest, I didn't have the energy to process how I felt about what she'd just told me. And, much like her AI, I lacked a relevant frame of reference. I rested my head on her shoulder and leant back against the wall, trying not to think about why it felt slick. Walls should not be slick. After what felt like an age, I fell asleep too.

———

I jerked awake when one of the orions banged on the cell door. Bexley sat up with a jolt and a noise that sounded unnervingly like 'Buffy'.

'Wakey, wakey,' said the slightly taller guard. 'Time to—' They made a motion with their three-fingered hand like a crashing ship or a falling stone. My stomach flipped.

The shorter, stockier guard grabbed Bexley by the arm and dragged her from the cell.

'Take your stinking paws off her, you twatting troll-doll,' I roared.

'Tell your pet to quit mewling,' the guard said to Bexley.

'Tell me yourself, arsewangle.'

Bexley turned her head to me and whispered, 'Don't start anything, Lem. Not now. Please.'

I nodded and moved to follow. The taller guard grabbed my arms and roughly twisted them behind my back. They knocked me down to my knees so they could reach up to slap one of those bags over my head. The last thing I saw as they did so was the other guard doing the same to Bexley. Together, they half marched, half dragged us out of the cell, turning left, away from the shuttle dock.

We went maybe fifty metres or so – me slipping and stumbling the whole way. I heard a door scrape open. The guard pushed me through. Someone scooped me up and dropped me into a pool of goo – presumably one of the pods.

I was praying to every god I'd ever heard of that this daft plan paid off. If it didn't, Bexley and I were going to be auctioned off as slaves.

I felt the restraints being fastened over my inert form. One of the orions pulled the hood-bag-thing off my head and slammed the pod door. Once again, I was in complete darkness. The only sounds were the rapid drumming of my heart and the Darth Vader mask sounds of my breathing.

'Here goes nothing,' I said to no one as the paralysis fugue faded. Then the sensory deprivation roller coaster started all over again. After that, there was only screaming.

Just when I'd convinced myself we'd been accidentally waylaid and I was drifting in open space, the door to my pod was yanked open. Spock leapt in and danced on my bladder while covering me in sloppy dog kisses.

'Lem! Lem back! Lem!' She wagged her tail so hard she fell right out of the pod. I took the opportunity to haul myself out of the pod.

I clutched my dog, gratefully. The greatest sense of relief I'd ever experienced washed over me. I felt like I could collapse to the floor right there in the transporter room and never move again. But there were still things to be done.

'Henry,' I said, reaching out a hand towards the robot who'd opened my pod door. I stopped myself before I touched her. Obviously. 'I've never been so happy to see you. Or, you know, anyone. Thank you.'

'All right, sandwich,' said Henry. 'Get over yourself. There's no need to get all emotional on me.'

I blinked back tears I refused to shed. 'Bexley still out cold?'

Henry waved a grabby tool in the direction of one of the

other pods. 'Yeah. Give her a minute. She should be fine.' By her standards, I reckoned this was the equivalent of Henry throwing us a welcome home banquet with a brass band and an eight-course dinner.

Once again, Bexley sprang from the pod and ran in frantic circles around the room. I flinched as she bounced off the walls in the tiny space. Spock leapt out of her way and Henry wheeled herself over to the door frame.

'We made it? We made it. Oh my gosh, we made it!' She put her arms on my waist and grabbed Henry's lid – I guess that's what you'd call it – and danced us around the room. Spock circled after us, nipping at Henry's wheels.

'Oh my gosh,' Bexley declared. 'I'm so hungry, I could eat a horse.'

I did a horrified double-take before I realised Holly was just translating her words into a familiar colloquialism and she probably wasn't threatening to become a cannibal.

'We could, er,' I stabbed a thumb in the direction of the kitchen, 'go see if Aurora can whip you something up.'

'I like the way you think, Lem.' She put her arm through mine and led me out of the room.

'Don't mind me,' said Henry. 'I'll just go back to the bridge to try to fly us out of this mess, shall I?'

'Hey,' I called out.

Henry stopped where she was, but didn't turn around. 'What is it, cheese puff?'

'Thank you,' I said. 'For rescuing us. You saved our lives.'

As she rolled away down the hall, she said, 'Don't mention it. Seriously, just don't. I have a reputation to maintain.'

I smiled at Bexley and we turned the corner into the kitchen.

Aurora had completely engulfed BB, who was shaking

violently and squawking strangely. Aurora glowed almost entirely orange.

'Doc, are you okay?' I ran to them and tried to help, but BB pulled away from me and fled into the lounge. I heard Bexley nicker. I turned back to the door to find Bexley and Spock both staring openly. Bexley's lips were pressed tightly together.

'What? What?' Bexley tilted her head to one side in a way that looked like it was supposed to mean something to me, but— 'Oh. Oh! Oh, bollocks, Aurora,' I mumbled. 'I'm so sorry. We didn't mean to ... interrupt ... anything.'

The moment the door slid shut behind BB, Bexley ran to Aurora and neighed. 'Aurora, I'm so happy for you two. That was sex, right? You two were getting, you know, jiggy with it. That's amazing. I'm so pleased for you! I know the peri can be super-private about things. How did you even— Oh, I'm just so happy for you both.'

Aurora glowed brilliant yellow. I hadn't worked out all her colours yet, but I'd put money on yellow being awkwardness or embarrassment. I stepped forwards and touched Bexley on the shoulder. 'Come on, give her – give both of them – some space.' I gently tugged Bexley towards myself then looked back at Aurora. 'I'm so sorry about that. We'll, er, come back in a bit, yeah? We've got to go get cleaned up anyway. Tell BB we're so sorry.'

I dragged Bexley out of the room, knowing Spock would follow.

'Where are we going?' asked Bexley. 'And why don't you want me to ask Aurora sex questions?'

'We're giving them privacy,' I replied as I stabbed the button to call the lift. 'Besides, we stink and we're covered in prison juice. We're going to our rooms to get cleaned up.' As we got into the lift, I added, 'Er, do you know where our rooms are from here?'

'Oh, yeah... While you were in the medlab, most of us moved up to the crew quarters. The rooms are a lot more comfy than the prison cells.'

The lift doors slid open on a level I hadn't been to before – no, wait... 'I think I've been on this level. This is where the bunnyboos interviewed me.'

Bexley stabbed a hoof-hand to the left. 'Yeah, the meeting room is that way.' She started walking in the opposite direction. 'Come on, I'll show you to the room we assigned you and you can tell me why you didn't want me talking to Aurora about sex.'

I had to jog a few steps to catch up with her as she headed into a room. 'It was pretty clear BB was horrified that we caught them.'

'Yeah, sure, I get that,' said Bexley as she spread her arms wide. 'This is your room, by the way. I told you how private the peri are. But I didn't ask BB about sex. I asked Aurora.'

I nodded absently as I looked around. 'Yeah, I get that. But Aurora was pretty clearly embarrassed on BB's behalf. Just imagine how horrified BB would be if she knew Aurora was in there chatting with us about something that's patently a deeply private thing for her.' My original pyjamas were neatly folded – and presumably clean – on the bed waiting for me.

'Oh, that's a really good point,' said Bexley. 'I hadn't considered that. Hey, do you want to shower together?'

Putting both my hands on her shoulders, I turned her around so she was facing the door. 'No. I'll meet you back in the lounge in twenty minutes. Go back and shower in your own room.'

She raised her hand-hooves in a very human gesture of

self-defence. 'Hey, I didn't mean for sex. I just meant we could help clean one another. But, yeah, sure. Twenty minutes sounds good. Weird number to pick, but okay.'

———

Spock got there before me and the doors to the lounge slid open. I winced, hoping BB wasn't still hiding in there. Instead, I found Bexley and Aurora.

'I swear I wasn't asking her *anything*,' Bexley declared as soon as she spotted me. 'Well, no. That's not true. I was asking her something. Just not about … that. I was making a request for something to eat. I don't know about you, but I'm absolutely famished.'

'I ate before I went … before everything. But I'd love a cup of tea, if that's okay, Aurora?'

Aurora glowed blue, but with a few streaks of emerald green. 'Of course, Lem. Was this morning's tea okay? Or should I change anything?'

I ran my hand through my hair. 'This morning? Did we … did you … oh wow – that was this morning? Today's been about four years long.' That explained how exhausted I felt. 'Yeah, that was perfect. Thank you.' *How long had it been since I last slept?*

Aurora headed into the kitchen to tend to things. I felt like I needed to say something to Bexley to fill the silence but I had no idea what.

'You got your blanket-armour back,' she said.

'Someone cleaned it for me. Aurora, I'd imagine.'

The silence hung awkwardly between us until Spock banished it by farting noisily. Bexley and I smiled at one another. 'Shall we sit?' I asked, feeling oddly formal.

She tapped her hand-hoof mid-air. We walked over to one

of the sofas and sat down next to one another. The furniture had been rearranged again. No more banishing Bexley and me to opposite ends of the room.

After a few awkward moments, the kitchen door slid open. Aurora drifted in with a floating tray of dishes – followed, somewhat unexpectedly, by BB. The featherless skin of her cheeks showed that slight blush.

'Hey, Doc,' I said.

'I'm so sorry we walked in on you,' Bexley said. 'We had no idea and we never would have —'

BB ground her beak. She looked like she was trying to say something, but I guessed the words were catching in her throat.

'It's we who should apologise to you,' said Aurora. 'You may have gathered by now that my relationship to BB is not... That is, it didn't begin when she was captured by the bunnyboos.'

'What?' I blinked back my shock.

'Yeah, no, for sure. I totally get that.' Bexley touched her hand-hoof to her forelock – hiding the remnants of her horn. 'Wait, what?'

BB removed the dishes from the tray and laid them out on the table. 'We should tell them, Aurora. We owe them the truth.'

Bexley jumped off the sofa. She lifted the lid off her dinner and tucked in. 'Sorry, I'm starving. Carry on, though – I want to hear this.'

I stood up, not sure where I was intending to go. 'Hang on. Shouldn't Henry hear this, too?'

'Henry knows all this. I'm the one who hired her.' BB handed me my mug of tea.

'Cheers,' I said for lack of words to express my confusion about everything they were saying. I sat back down on the sofa. Spock jumped up next to me and went to sleep. She'd obviously decided that this didn't concern her. Or maybe she just wasn't bothered one way or another.

Since no one else seemed to be saying anything, I prodded the conversation along. 'When you say you hired her…'

Aurora floated to where BB was standing but refrained from touching her. 'What I told you before about falling on hard times and signing up to work for the bunnyboos … that was true. But my contract was up fourteen months ago.'

BB clucked her beak. 'Aurora and I have been married for six and a half years. And for almost half that time, we've had no contact with one another. They promised she would be returned to me at the end of her contract. Instead … nothing. In desperation, I searched everywhere. Absolutely everywhere. I got little snippets of gossip here and rumours of things there. But rarely anything concrete, and never in time for me to act.'

BB climbed up onto a perch in a corner of the room that I swear wasn't previously there. She sighed dramatically and fluffed her feathers out. 'Because she had willingly signed the contract, the judoon wouldn't help. There didn't seem to be anything I could do.'

Someone had mentioned the judoon before, but I couldn't remember when. They must be the space police. Bexley finished her dinner and returned to sit with me on the sofa. I squeezed her leg gently and she returned the gesture.

'Eventually, in desperation, I gave birth to a plan. I knew the bunnyboos sometimes acted as bounty hunters, so I hired a hacker—'

Both Bexley and I shouted out at once. 'Henry!'

Spock woke up and glared at us. 'Rude,' she said before falling back asleep.

'Indeed, as you have correctly deduced, it was Henry I hired. Together, we chose a few individuals we thought would be amenable to helping. Then Henry sent an irresistible message to the bunnyboos, offering them sizeable bounties on the people we'd chosen in the hopes they'd take the bait.'

Bexley leant forwards in her seat and quivered with excitement. 'So, I was never really charged with—' She glanced around the room. 'Oh, phew! That's amazing. I was really freaking out about that. I mean, I would never— Um, anyways. And then you planted a ruse to lure them away, so that Henry could crack us all out. That's brilliant!'

BB tilted her head to the side. 'Yes, well, it hasn't quite gone off without a hitch. Quite a few factors didn't exactly go to plan.' She glanced in my direction before quickly looking away.

'Me,' I said. 'I wasn't part of this plan. I don't fit in. Or Spock for that matter. I mean, it's obvious why BB's here. And Henry. And, Bexley, you're, like, a genius mechanic who just happens to know every detail of this class of ship and how to keep it running.'

'That is true.' BB danced from foot to foot.

I bit my lip. 'A warrior, that's what Henry said, right? Some warrior I turned out to be?'

'I passed details of the individuals I had selected to Henry, who passed them—'

BB's words were cut off by the door swooshing open and Henry rolling in. 'And I passed them to the bunnyboos – those kumquats stuffed with hay. They cooked everything up and brought us these two useless lumps of under-proved dough, instead of the warriors we told them to pick up.'

'Right,' I said – unsure of whether I ought to be insulted or relieved.

Bexley leapt up off the sofa for about the hundredth time and ran to BB, throwing her arms around the embarrassed parrot. 'I guess, please don't kidnap me again, but I'm just so glad you got your spouse back.'

The room flashed purple and an alarm sounded. Everyone's translators spoke at once. 'Proximity alert. Proximity alert.'

Henry rolled out of the room faster than I would have imagined her little wheels could carry her, but Holly brought her words right to me. 'It's the decking bunnyboos. Bexley, if you can work any voodoo that will get us to warp with dead dilithium crystals, now would be a really good time to mention it.'

Bexley was galloping for the engine room. 'I'm on it. I'll find a way to squeeze some juice out of them.'

Spock and I ran after her. When we got to the engine room, she ducked into the toilet. She didn't shut the door, so I ducked in after her.

She held a razor blade to her forehead. 'There's nothing there,' she shrieked. 'I can't get blood from a stone – if you see what I mean.'

I had an idea. 'Is there a nail file or some sandpaper anywhere?'

'Yeah.' She reached into the drawer under the sink and handed me a large emery board. 'But it's no good. There's no growth. I already dug into the base of the horn to get us to Magrathea.'

'Come with me. I've got a theory.' I ran to the engine and yanked out the dilithium drawer. 'Give me your, er, hand-hoof. Please. Please give me your hand.'

She held a hand out over the drawer and looked at me questioningly. 'Okay, I don't get what you're doing right now.'

'Nails are made of the same material as bone, right? Broadly speaking,' I said without the first clue as to whether it was true. 'Like, maybe not exactly the same, but similar, right?' I held the file to her hand and rubbed it back and forth. The first pale flakes of powdered hoof fell into the drawer. I kept going. After a minute, I was rewarded with tiny pinpricks of colour that appeared in the washing powder.

'Wha— Ha ha!' After that, we were both just neighing, whinnying, squealing, and hooting – as dictated by our respective physiologies. Spock got in on the action too, dancing in circles around us and barking excitedly.

Bexley slammed the drawer shut. 'You've got crystals, Henry. Hit it. Get us the crap out of here.'

'On it.'

'We didn't get very much, but we got you some,' Bexley added. 'Should be enough to get us—' She tapped a hoof in the air like she was typing on a calculator. 'It should get us about twelve minutes at warp four.'

'I don't know what kind of tucking wizardry you had to pull to get any life into those scabby crystals, but I don't give a shin. We are at warp four.'

Bexley looked at me, her eyes and nostrils wide. 'I had no idea that would work. It wasn't as effective as powdered horn, but that stuff is, like' – she made an expansive gesture with her whole arms – 'super-powerful. I'm guessing maybe there's a lower percentage of the unobtainium in my hooves than there is in my horn. That would make a really—'

'Bexley,' I said impatiently. 'Will they be able to follow us?'

Bexley ran back into the bathroom and returned with a towel. 'That depends on how close attention they were paying when we went into warp.' She dropped into a sitting position on the floor. 'Now help me work on my feet. I told Henry twelve minutes. But we're going to need a lot more filings than we've got so far if we're going to last that long.'

Once we'd fed the dilithium chamber all the hoof filings we could get without hurting Bexley, we ran up to the bridge to see if we could help.

'I think we're clear,' said Henry as the lift doors opened. 'I've been dropping us out of warp, changing course, and then going back to warp. We're going to run out of fuel soon, but – digits crossed – I think we've lost them.'

Spock, as always when she was on the bridge, headed straight for the big window. 'Walkies?'

'Not now,' I said. 'Sorry, sweetie.'

Bexley ran to the station next to Henry's. 'What can we do?'

It was a bizarre scene to witness. Henry had a cable extended from her torso that plugged into the dashboard in front of her, yet aside from that – she looked like an abandoned rubbish bin in the middle of the space. As if some futuristic cleaner had been called away while they were hoovering the bridge of a starship.

'For lack of a better idea, I've just been picking random directions as headings,' said Henry. 'I didn't spot the bunnyboos at our last few stops, so – cross everything you've got – I think we might be in the clear.'

We all held our breath for a moment. Figuratively, at least.

'And we're back in normal space,' said Henry, rolling back from the pilot's station. 'That was the last of the dilithium. We're just floating in open space now. Looks like we're about fourteen months from Trantor. Without FTL, we'll get there eventually.'

'Oh, excellent,' Bexley said.

I rubbed my jaw. 'What? How is that excellent? In what way is fourteen months drifting through space' – my hands were waving themselves around of their own accord – 'towards some random planet anyone's definition of an "excellent" outcome?'

No one responded so I kept going. 'Look, it's all I can do to keep myself from having a complete mental breakdown. I'm stressed out and tired and hungry. I want to go home.' The last word was little more than a whimper.

Bexley ran to me and put her arms around my waist. 'Hey, hey, hey. It's excellent because it means we're heading into a major shipping lane. If we just coast and we don't run into anyone, we'll get to Trantor – which, by the way, is the seat of galactic government – eventually. But it also means there will be other ships passing. We can communicate with them and they can sell us some unobtainium, or at least send help. It won't be long. We'll send out a distress beacon and any ship that passes by will pick it up.'

I sniffed. 'So, we're safe?' I swallowed down the rising bile.

She flicked her head. 'Looks that way – at least for now.' She took a step away and grabbed my hand. 'Come on, we'll go down to the kitchen and get you a drink.'

I took a deep breath. 'I'd like that.'

She turned back to face Henry. 'You can handle things from here, yeah? Lem and Spock and I are going to take a quick breather.'

'Oh no,' Henry said dryly, 'how ever will I manage to pilot this almost entirely automated ship all by my scabbing self?'

The lift doors swished open. The three of us stepped in just as Holly announced, 'Proximity alert. Proximity alert.' The whole bridge lit up purple.

I threw my hands up. 'What now?'

Bexley moved like lightning. Before I knew it, she was back across the bridge with Henry. 'What is it? What are we picking up?'

'Goat puckers,' said Henry. 'It's the cuffing bunnyboos.'

'What do we—' Before I could finish that needless sentence, something rocked us. I wasn't holding on to anything so I landed on my arse. Bexley caught her forehead on one of the station dashboards. Spock and Henry seemed more stable. 'What the hell was that?'

Bexley's hands raced over the station she had collided with. 'Uh oh.' Her next words were shouted with an urgency I felt in my bones. 'BB, Aurora, get to the starbug docking port. Do not let those jackasses board us.'

She grabbed my arm and pulled me back towards the lift. 'We're on our way to give backup. Henry, do what you can to lock them out from here.'

As the lift door closed, I looked at her, seeing her afresh. 'That was seriously impressive. You just went from the chatty, bubbly Bexley I know, to this — I don't know — military school headmistress or CEO.'

She crossed her arms over her chest and I actually took a step backwards away from her. But the grin she flashed was pure Bexley. 'I know, right? Four terms of command college will do that to you. Isn't it amazing?'

I nodded mutely.

'BB, Aurora, sit-rep. What's your status?'

It seemed she could turn it on and off on a dime. 'Gobsmacked,' I muttered.

'Little busy here,' said Aurora.

When the lift doors opened, Bexley and Spock raced off. I lumbered after them, following in their wake through the cargo bay where Aurora had brought me – *was it really only a few hours ago? That didn't seem right.*

We headed the opposite direction from the door I'd used when we'd docked with Terok Nor. Spock and Bexley skidded to a halt outside an open door. Bexley motioned for me to come closer but to stay quiet.

Around the corner, on the other side of the door, I heard movement.

'Sounds like the bastards boarded us,' I whispered.

Bexley shot me a look that could wrinkle a raisin, once again channelling that commanding attitude. I'd have to find out more about this. It was almost like she swapped out personalities. 'Later. I know,' I muttered. 'This isn't the time.' I tried to focus on the problem at hand.

'Five ducking bunnyboos just boarded the *Teapot*,' said Henry – still safely ensconced on the bridge.

'Great, they've brought the whole rainbow.'

Bexley glared at me again, but I just couldn't help it. I was on a spaceship in the middle of nowhere, being attacked by a squad of pastel-coloured, vicious, intelligent bunnies. Well, okay, maybe the intelligent bit was a stretch. 'How in the hell has my life come to this?'

'Can you be quiet, please?' Bexley whisper-snapped. 'I'm trying to strategise.'

The bunnyboos came through the door and it was on.

There was no way I was going to let these overgrown jackrabbits take me again.

No sooner had the purple grunt passed through the door than Spock was sailing through the air, snarling, teeth bared. 'Kill the wabbit!'

Wabbit? Seriously? demanded some distant part of my brain.

Purple screamed and tried to run the other way, but Spock was fast. She chomped down on bunnyboo arse like it was her last meal. Purple ran this way and that, trying to shake Spock off, but she held on, teeth firmly stuck into Purple's bum.

That left Bexley and me to face down the blue boss and a massive bunnyboo I'd not met before. Peachy coloured with brilliant orange eyes.

Well, massive is relative – she maybe stood as high as my chin. But she had the arms of a pro wrestler.

Purple appeared to be losing her battle with Spock.

The bunnyboos were each equipped with those tranq weapons they'd shot me with back in the dawn of time. And I had … nothing.

Bexley hefted a – was that a toilet brush? It sure looked like a toilet brush. *Where did she get a toilet brush?* She waved it at the bunnyboos.

Whatever it was, it seemed to scare them – they all ducked behind the sliding door. They used the cover to fire tranqs at us.

It went on like that for a bit. The bunnyboos tried to knock us out. Bexley smashed any exposed fingers with her strange makeshift weapon.

And I slung jokes and insults like ninja stars. 'If I give you some carrots, will you leave us alone?'

'Why would we want plant roots?' replied Blue.

That just made me want to hit them even more. *Stupid bunnies*. Then, things got serious.

I had just delivered another brilliant insult when there was a thump, a crunch, and a yelp from down the hall. That sound… I knew that sound and it killed me.

I saw Spock on the floor, unmoving. Her upper body was a bloody, pulpy mess.

I didn't even see what Purple had done. My vision filled with red. I had to do something.

So, I did the only logical thing that I could do.

I looked around for something that would serve as a weapon. I spotted something that looked like a frying pan. *Good heft*. I flung it at the purple creep, hitting the mangled mess of her arse.

Purple fell to the floor, screaming silently.

Good.

'You killed my best friend, you fuzzy little bastards. I'll kill every last one of you, you monsters.' I launched myself at the nearest bunnyboo, whichever arsehole it was.

The last thing I saw was a weapon being pointed at me. Then something hit me and I died. Again. *This had better not turn out to be habit-forming*.

I wasn't dead, but I was warm and comfortable, so I decided to stay in bed a bit longer. Somewhere, at the edge of my memory, I recalled a strange dream. *What was it about?*

Without opening my eyes, I mumbled, 'Ugh, Spock. You're not going to believe the dream I had.'

Behind me, a voice whispered, 'Now, don't panic.'

I jumped out of bed, in a panic. 'Bollocks!' I was back in my prison cell on the *Teapot*. 'Bexley! What the hell are you doing in my bed? Where's Spock? What happened?'

'Hey, I said don't freak out. This sure looks like you freaking out.' She was curled up on her side, her mane splayed out, covering her face. Weirdly, the thing I found most disconcerting was that, although her words seemed to be mumbled and were probably only semi-coherent, Holly translated them into crystal-clear English.

'Don't tell me to not panic, Bexley,' I said. 'Why the hell wouldn't I freak out? Because my dog and I have now been kidnapped several times apiece and now she's been murdered by alien bunnies and I'm in a prison with my best friend telling me not to panic. What's there to not freak out about?'

Bexley sat up in bed and studied me, her nostrils flaring as she sniffed the air. 'Wow, that is so bizarre. Normally, I hear you speak before my AI translates your words. But this time all I could hear was the translation. Like, I could see your funny little mouth moving, but I didn't hear anything coming out of it. Were you actually speaking there?'

'What?'

She shifted positions so she could see me more easily. 'Oh, weird. I heard that one. Oh, I wonder if I only hear one end of your vocal range. Do you think you were speaking at a higher pitch or a lower one?'

'What?' I waved my hands to dismiss the thought. 'No, don't answer that. Bexley, what the hell is going on? What happened? And before you ask again, it was higher. When I'm stressed out, I speak at a higher pitch. It's a human thing. Well, an Earth thing. Spock does the same.'

'Oh, interesting. I wonder what the mechanics behind that are. BB could probably— Okay, fine, fine. After Spock attacked and that purple bastard hit her with whatever, you went kamikaze on their asses. It was – I mean, okay, I'll be honest – you're not the greatest fighter, but the thing is you gave it *everything*. Like, you jumped on top of Purple and put her in a headlock. She was spinning around and around trying to get you off, but she couldn't. You bit down on her ear – I think you actually tore it.'

I had thought the furry sensation in my mouth was figurative, not literal. *Could I taste blood?* Smacking my tongue, I ran for the bathroom. When I finished being sick, I rinsed my mouth out and gulped down several handfuls of lukewarm water.

I returned to the cell and climbed back into bed. Bexley looked at me curiously. 'Are you okay?'

I nodded. 'Yes. No. I'm not sure. I want to go home. What happened to Spock?'

She touched my shoulder. 'I think it was just a shoulder wound. Last I heard, BB was operating on her. Aurora said she'd try to bring word with our dinners.'

'Oh, thank God.'

Bexley pulled me to herself and held me tight. We lay there for a bit, snuggled up close in our alien prison cell. 'You were amazing,' she said eventually. 'Green had to hit you with that tranq thing to get you off Purple. You were never going to let go.'

I sat up. 'How's everyone else? Are you okay?'

She touched a hoof to a bandage I hadn't even noticed. 'It's okay. They must've let Doc stitch me up after I got tranqed.'

I touched my forehead. My muscles were knotted up, tight. 'You got shot?'

Bexley tapped the air. 'Yeah, maybe a minute after you did. Only woke up a couple hours ago. I think they put us together because they mixed up me and Spock.'

My jaw fell open. 'What? They think you're my dog?'

Bexley made a strange sort of grimace-neigh. 'I'm not a pet. They think you're *my* pet.'

'I'm not a pet,' I said.

'Well, I'm not a pet either,' she repeated.

'What are we going to do now?' I leant back against her. 'Hey, hang on. Shouldn't I be reacting to you by now? If not now, then soon, surely. I should probably get away from you before BB's drug wears off.' I scrambled to the other side of the room. 'Just to be safe. I don't want to die and all that.'

'No, no, I totally get that,' she said.

'Oh, relax, sandwich,' said a voice from my watch. 'BB

dosed you with the drug before they brought you back to the cell.'

'Henry!' exclaimed both Bexley and I together.

'The one and only.'

I looked around. 'Where are you?'

'Did you seriously just look for me in your prison cell? Like you might not have noticed me in there before? Maybe sitting in the corner, all unobtrusive-like? Possibly behind a pot plant.'

'Pff! No,' I said. 'As if. Of course not.' I glanced sideways at Bexley.

'Oh relax, you two. It's not like I've been watching the CCTV footage of your cell all night. Not that I'd have seen anything interesting anyway.'

'Henry!'

'Since you're obviously still hacked into the ship's systems,' Bexley said, 'can you at least tell us what's going on?'

'Well, for starters, you can thank me for why you two are sharing. I swapped out Bexley and Spock's profiles, so now they think you are Spock – who is fine, by the way. She's out of surgery but still under anaesthetic. The doc is monitoring her.'

'Oh, thank God,' I said, nearly collapsing under the weight of my guilt.

'I am also fine,' said Henry. 'I'm in the cell to the left of yours. Not that you cheeseballs cared enough to ask after my well-being, obviously. But I figured you should know. I frocked a couple of them up before they got me. Aurora's okay, too. She managed to persuade the idiot bunnyboos that we had taken her hostage.'

'But now we're back where we started,' I moaned.

Bexley got up and frantically paced around the room.

'That's true in a sense. But also, when you think about it, we've got a lot more information than we did the first time around. We know who we are, not just as individuals, I mean – we also know each other. And we know why we're here. If we work together, surely we can come—'

Holly cut her words off. 'Proximity alert. Proximity alert.'

I groaned. 'Oh, what now? How many more—'

Bexley reversed course, circling the room in the other direction. 'I thought all the bunnyboos were here already, no?'

'As far as I can tell,' said Henry's disembodied voice.

'Then who the hell—' I began.

Bexley looked at me, nostrils flaring. 'The orions? Would they come after us?'

'Attention, crew of the starship *Teapot*,' said a new voice from my watch. 'This is the Captain of the *Dayus X*, representing the judoon space force. You will surrender your vessel and prepare to be boarded.' I had Holly's figurative mode and my own geek-culture-soaked brain for that whopper of a mixed metaphor.

'You are accused of six counts of kidnapping and false imprisonment, as well as two counts of aggravated assault and one attempted murder.'

There was a gentle thud – not at all like the violent collision when the bunnyboos slammed into us last night.

'Oh, yeah,' said Henry – sounding inordinately pleased with herself. 'Did I mention? I also called the cops.'

I waited for Spock in the tastefully appointed family lounge in the galactic courthouse on Trantor. Like a nervous parent, I paced the halls outside the room where Spock was being held. I'd given my final deposition this morning and now it was her turn. They were unlikely to get much out of her. Her memory of anything beyond a few minutes ago was pretty shaky.

I touched the soft fabric of my dress. A few of the species that called Trantor home wore clothes. The representative assigned to me had helped me seek out a tailor in a nearby market. I had three new dresses – all pretty, flattering, amazingly comfy, and with plenty of well-placed pockets. The seller had assured me they were all up to the minute in stylistic terms too. I still wore the shoes Bexley made me, though.

'Oh my gosh. I love your— Are those scales? They really bring out your eye.' I got up and ran towards the voice I'd have known anywhere. 'Hey listen, the person at the front desk told me to come to this floor, but I can't— Lem! Oh my gosh, oh my gosh! I can't believe it's been three whole days. I missed you so much.' She skidded to a halt a couple of metres away. 'Hang on, are you…'

I chuckled. 'I'm medicated, yes.' I opened my arms to embrace her and she ran straight for me, almost crushing me with the ferocity of her hug.

After a few minutes, she pulled back. 'Is Spock not finished yet?'

I shook my head. 'Feels like she's been in there for ages. I'm worried about her.'

She stroked my shoulder. 'Don't be. She can take it.'

'I know. But I'm so glad they let us stay together these last few days.' We'd all been sequestered and everyone else had been split up so we could be questioned separately. But, in between debriefing sessions, Spock and I were allowed to be together.

'Of course, silly,' said Bexley. 'You're her left hand. It would be inhumane to keep you apart.'

'Her left hand?'

'Yeah, you know,' she said. 'The person who supports you and makes sure you're where you need to be and all that? It's like the person who stands on your non-dominant side to ensure you're fully covered.'

'I like that. I'm her left hand.'

We both turned towards the noise as a door clicked open. Spock stepped out, holding her brain toy, followed by three other people, all of different species. She walked calmly and deliberately – until she spotted us. Then all decorum went out the window.

Spock ran over, wagging her tail and dancing. She squeaked her brain gleefully before dumping it unceremoniously at my feet. 'Friend Bexley! Spock missed Bexley!'

Bexley dropped to all fours – wiggling and wrestling with Spock.

I turned to the officer in charge of the deposition. 'Are we all done here?'

The person, a three-metre-tall lizard-spider-something, clicked her many digits. 'We are finished. You are all free to leave. Thanks to your cooperation, I expect the bunnyboos will be in rehabilitation for quite some time.'

Bexley stood up and brushed herself off.

Spock finally noticed me and licked my hand. 'Lem! Wanna go home.'

'I know, mate.' I wiped her slobber off on her head. 'Soon, but not yet.' The thought of going home – finally – felt too good to be true. We'd had the adventure of a lifetime. But there's no place like home and all that. Yet, I wasn't quite ready to say goodbye to my new friends.

'Not home?' Her big, sad eyes would have had me caving in to any demand. Except...

'Not home,' Bexley said. 'First, we're going to go for dinner. Then we'll get you home.'

Spock's eyes lit up. 'Dinner? Feed Spock?'

The three of us headed out of the building as the alien suns began to set. The sunsets on Trantor glowed green and purple. It was like pictures I'd seen of the northern lights – but every single day and visible from everywhere. I'd always wanted to see the northern lights.

I put my hand through Bexley's elbow. The height difference made it only slightly awkward, but it still felt right. 'Where to, boss?'

She looked up at me and grinned. 'I know just the place: the White Hart. The others are going to meet us there.'

I was getting more used to the transporters. Spock still didn't like them, but even she was more comfortable with them. Bexley, though ... was still Bexley.

A few minutes after we arrived on the station orbiting Trantor, she leapt out of her pod and did her whole thing of running around like a kid on a sugar rush. 'Whoa, whoa, whoa.'

I struggled not to giggle. Eventually, I'd have to tell her about horses. Maybe.

When she'd collected herself, Bexley led us through the maze of a station to a building that was – even to my naïve alien eyes – clearly a pub. Inside, there was the usual collection of assorted furniture designed for various species. In the far corner, three familiar faces greeted us. Well, not faces so much. Three people. But only one with a face. BB lifted her wings in welcome.

Spock, Bexley, and I waved and then headed to the bar to order. 'Is there anything vaguely beer-like here?'

'You want fermented grain juice?' Bexley asked.

'Hang on, it's not going to be, like, lumpy or slimy or served in a bowl, is it?'

She flicked her head. 'Do you want it that way?'

I raised both my hands in alarm. 'No, definitely not.'

We managed to convey our orders and pay. Then we headed for the table with the others. Spock went straight under the table. She was snoozing within seconds.

'So you successfully convinced them you weren't hardened criminals, then, meatsacks?'

'The drug I created for you is still working, I take it?'

'I'm off the ship! Can you believe it? I'm still so excited I've been telling everyone I've met for three days now.'

'Henry, BB, Aurora,' I said, acknowledging each one with a nod. 'And, yes, Doc... Still does the trick. I haven't taken more than one of your magic antihistamine a day since I had my first dose.'

'Aurora,' squealed Bexley. 'I'm so delighted for you. It must be amazing to finally be free. What was the first thing you did when the judoon freed you?'

Aurora glowed sort of purple or blue – though it was harder to tell in the pub's dim lighting. 'Well, yes. It is, indeed. But also, that ship has come to feel like home over the past few years. It does feel a bit overwhelming to know I can't go home again. I don't know. That sounds weird to admit.'

Bexley clapped her hand-hooves together excitedly. 'That's what I wanted to tell you all! I bought the ship!'

'You…' said Aurora.

BB clucked her beak. 'Bought…'

'The *Teapot*…' said Henry.

I faced Bexley, mouth agape. 'You bought the *Teapot*?'

Bexley tapped the tabletop in front of herself and grinned her massive grin. 'Well, one of my dads did. She owns the company that makes the engines. Did I never tell you that? We're super-rich.' She brushed her forelock down over her face. 'Yeah, I dunno. I had such a good time with you all that … well, I mean … I thought maybe —'

I burst out laughing. Only Bexley could find the fun side of being kidnapped.

———

After a hearty meal – and more drinks than I could count – we all left the pub and walked to the landing dock. My jaw fell slack as I looked out the massive window.

'Itch taped,' I slurred. 'I mean, it's paished. Iz a teapot! Zatshly a teapot.'

Spock wagged her tail.

Bexley, who seemed way more sober than she had any right to be, said, 'Yeah, the *Teapot*. I told you I bought it. Didn't you believe me?'

'No, I did. 'Course I did,' I said. 'But ss shaped like a teapot. Iz a normous, colossive teapot. A bigly foo … fush … hop tink … pink teapot.'

She clicked a button on her medallion and a ramp swung down. Spock ran up it and turned back to wait for us. Bexley helped me up the ramp – I would have fallen off it without her support.

'Home,' cried Spock. She danced in precarious circles at the top of the ramp.

'I know, mate.' I leant on the door frame and looked out at the strange lights of the strange new universe – some of which were blurring together. 'I said we'd go home.'

Something finally clicked. I'd spent so much time thinking about going home, that I'd completely forgotten to think about what home actually was – what the word even meant. I'd not felt at home on Earth for a long time. For that matter, how long had it been since I'd even felt at home in my own skin?

Bexley took me by the arm and pulled me into the ship as Spock ran in circles around us. The others trailed us not far behind.

'No,' said my dog. 'Are home.'

THE END (FOR NOW)

Lem and the whole *Teapot* crew will be back in 2022. Sign up to my newsletter to get updates. And you'll get free stories as well.

If you'd like to read about Lem's life on Earth – including how she first met Spock – click below.

PSST! WANT A FREE BOOK?

Click the image above to get Stardust Wake for free

ACKNOWLEDGEMENTS

It'd be strange to write an acknowledgements section in a novel right now without acknowledging the biggest event in recent history. But in this case, it would be virtually impossible to do so.

Towards the end of 2020, having handed over *Livid Skies* to my copy-editor, I sat down to write the third instalment in the *White Hart* series. But I could not get my brain to cooperate. With everything going on [she gestures wildly at the world], I just … couldn't. I couldn't face another serious novel about serious people dealing with serious problems.

Also, funny thing… It turns out that people aren't really all that into reading about the trauma of living in a post-pandemic world when they're living in the throes of an actual pandemic.

And so instead, I sat down to write something excessively silly. Something that would amuse me and take my mind off the horrors of the real world. I cracked out a first draft in six weeks and passed it over to a few beta readers.

Perhaps not all that surprisingly, readers seemed much

more receptive to ridiculous, absurd, uplifting science fiction than they were to traumatic pandemic fiction. Who knew?

Anyways... One of my earliest readers was Tyler Hayes. I once described Tyler's novel, *The Imaginary Corpse*, as part cosy mystery, part urban fantasy, part trippy-cheese-dream. If you enjoyed *The Left Hand of Dog* (or even if you wanted to but didn't), you should definitely check out *The Imaginary Corpse*. If you didn't enjoy my book and you think speculative fiction has a responsibility to take itself seriously ... well, then you probably won't like Tyler's book either.

Anyways... I met Tyler via Romancing the Runoff, the auction held by a group of romance authors to raise funds for the Georgia runoff election in the US in January 2021. Together, we played a tiny role in helping to flip America's senate. And I got some fab feedback that helped me shape this novel. Win-win!

The WiFi Sci-Fi writers' group has been the most amazing gift. They continually teach, push, and cheerlead me to be a better writer. As always, Genevieve Zander dug into the guts of my ridiculous tale – revealing the flaws, drawing out the details I'd invariably glossed over, and asking me all the right questions.

I've worked with a few different cover designers, but when I was writing this book, I knew stock art wasn't going to cut it. Weirdly, there just weren't any stock photos of day-glow pink spaceships shaped like teapots. Who could have predicted? I set out to find an artist, researching science fiction art. The same name kept popping up. Tom Edwards. I messaged him – and I'm so glad I did. I mean, have you seen the glorious, ridiculous, completely unique cover image he created for this book?

I'm phenomenally grateful to have such a great editing team. My first stop in editing this book was Lucy Rose York.

Lucy dug into the meat of this vegetarian story to make it the best version of itself it could be.

Nick Taylor at Just Write Right provided expert copy-editing services. I mostly write in British English these days, but I sometimes slip back into Canadianisms without realising it – which is fine when my characters are Canadian, but not so fine when they're not.

As always, Hannah McCall of Black Cat Editorial Services provided expert proofreading. Any mistakes you find now are because I forgot to incorporate her corrections.

Finally, legally contracted lifemate, Dave, has been putting up with more than any human being should ever have to. He's listened to me talk about Devon every single day for more than three years – and now I've added Lem to my little collection. Dave's awesome.

Photo © Lex Fleming

SI CLARKE is a misanthrope who lives in Deptford, *sarf ees* London. She shares her home with her partner and an assortment of waifs and strays. When not writing convoluted, inefficient stories, she spends her time telling financial services firms to behave more efficiently. When not doing either of those things, she can be found in the pub or shouting at people online – occasionally practising efficiency by doing both at once.

As someone who's neurodivergent, an immigrant, and the proud owner of an invisible disability, she strives to present a realistically diverse array of characters in her stories.

twitter.com/clacksee

goodreads.com/clacksee

ALSO BY SI CLARKE

Find a complete list of my books on my website at whitehartfiction.co.uk/books.

If you get books directly from me, you'll get 20% off with the code 'LEFTHAND'.

REVIEWS

If you enjoyed this story, please consider leaving a review on Goodreads, StoryGraph, or the ebook retailer of your choosing.

KEEP IN TOUCH

Join my newsletter for:

- snippets from what I'm working on;
- photos of my dogs;
- reviews of books I've enjoyed recently;
- links to promos with other authors (including free books); and
- free stories from me.

whitehartfiction.co.uk/newsletter-2